Ghost Stories Around the Campfire . . . with Real Ghosts?

All Lizzy Caldwell wants is to belong to a scout troop, so she's very happy when she gets an invitation from the Camp Fear Girls. An invitation that promises lots of spooky, scary fun.

But things might be getting too scary for Lizzy. Especially when she finds out the girls' clubhouse is on Fear Street— the spookiest place in the world.

And that Camp Fear Girls have a strange way of mysteriously disappearing. . . .

Also from R. L. Stine

The Beast
The Beast 2

R. L. Stine's Ghosts of Fear Street

Available from MINSTREL Books

R·L·STINE'S
GHOSTS of FEAR STREET ®

CAMP FEAR GHOULS

A Parachute Press Book

A
MINSTREL®
BOOK

Published by POCKET BOOKS
New York   London   Toronto   Sydney   Tokyo   Singapore

A MINSTREL PAPERBACK *Original*

 A Minstrel Paperback published by
POCKET BOOKS, a division of Simon & Schuster Inc.
1230 Avenue of the Americas, New York, NY 10020

Copyright © 1997 by Parachute Press, Inc.

CAMP FEAR GHOULS WRITTEN BY JAHNNA N. MALCOLM

ISBN: 0-671-00191-4

First Minstrel Books paperback printing March 1997

10 9 8 7 6 5 4 3 2 1

Cover art by Broeck Steadman

Printed in the U.S.A.

R·L·STINE'S
GHOSTS of FEAR STREET®

CAMP FEAR GHOULS

1

"**L**izzy, I'm scared!" Caroline Hurt whispered. She dug her fingers into my arm. "My hands are shaking!"

We pushed through the crowded school hallway. "Caroline, relax!" I ordered my best friend. "We're going to get in. Everybody says so."

I wished I felt as sure as I sounded. For two days I had barely been able to eat. Or sleep.

Why? Because today was the day the Waynesbridge Scouts—the coolest scout troop in Waynesbridge Middle School—picked their new members.

"I heard they slipped the invitations into the lockers last period. They're in pink envelopes," Caroline whispered. She ran her fingers through her short blond hair. Then she tugged down her favorite navy blue T-shirt. I knew she wanted to make sure she looked good for the big moment.

I tightened the scrunchie holding my straight brown hair. I might as well look good too, I thought. Even if it was just to open my locker and look for a pink envelope.

"It's not that big a deal," I told Caroline, trying to sound like I didn't really care.

But of course, I did. At Waynesbridge Middle School, every girl who's anybody is a Waynesbridge Scout. It's like a popularity contest. If you're picked, you're cool. If you're not picked—well, then you're a loser.

That's why we were so nervous.

Usually, I'm not that into the kinds of things the Waynesbridge Scouts do. You know. Fixing each other's hair and talking about boys. Caroline likes that stuff. I prefer softball. Camping. Climbing trees.

Most of all, I'm into scary stuff. Like ghost stories and monsters and horror movies.

But I'm definitely *not* into being a loser. So I was ready to do whatever it took to be a good Waynesbridge Scout.

Caroline clutched my arm. We shoved toward our lockers.

"Oh, Lizzy, what if we didn't make it? We'll be total losers! No one will ever talk to us again!" Caroline moaned and grabbed her stomach. "Ohhhh! I think I'm going to throw up!"

"Don't," I ordered.

2

Caroline and I have been best friends since the first grade. She's older than me. Nine whole months older. And taller by three inches. But she can be a total wimp. Whenever she's nervous, she threatens to throw up.

People tease me about being the shortest kid in the whole seventh grade. It makes me mad. But that's why Caroline and I are best friends. She has always stuck up for me.

Finally, we stopped in front of our lockers. They stood right next to each other.

"I can't go first," Caroline whimpered. "You do it, Lizzy."

"Why don't we open them at the same time?" I suggested.

"Good idea," Caroline agreed. "On the count of three."

We spun the combinations on our locks.

This is it, I thought. My heart thudded in my chest. I squeezed my eyes closed and counted in a shaky voice. "One, two—"

"Three!" we said together.

We flung our doors open and stared in.

"Yes!" Caroline shrieked. She pumped her fist in the air. "It's here! It's here!"

I searched through my locker. My backpack, my baseball cap, a couple of overdue library books, and my gym suit sat inside.

But nothing else.

No pink envelope.

No invitation to the Waynesbridge Scouts.

"I didn't make it," I whispered. I stared blankly into my locker.

Caroline clutched her pastel pink invitation to her chest. "Oh, Lizzy, it *has* to be there." She got down on her knees and tossed all my stuff out of the locker. She used only one hand. She held her own invitation tightly in the other.

In seconds, my locker was completely empty. But still—no pink envelope.

"No way. This has to be a mistake," Caroline insisted.

But I knew the awful truth. "It's no mistake," I said. "I wasn't asked to join. And I know why."

Caroline glanced up at me. "Why?"

"Arden Sitwell," I growled. My lip curled into a snarl. "Arden's mother is the scout leader. And Arden hates me for not inviting her to my birthday party last year."

Caroline's eyes widened. "You think Arden kept you out of the club for *that?*"

"It has to be."

Behind me I could hear the giggles of the Waynes-bridge Scouts. I turned to look at them.

Arden had perfect chin-length blond hair. She stood right in the middle of the scouts. They talked and laughed loudly.

"We'll show them," I murmured, narrowing my eyes at Arden. "We don't need their stupid club. We'll

4

form our own club. It will be way cooler than the Waynesbridge Scouts. Right?"

I waited for Caroline to agree with me, but she didn't say a word. Instead, she began placing things back in my locker.

"Right, Caroline?" I repeated, tapping her on the shoulder. "We'll form our own club. Right?"

Caroline stopped. She stared down at the pink envelope in her hand. "Listen, Lizzy," she mumbled. "I've wanted to be a Waynesbridge Scout since I was six. It means a lot to me."

"Well, it meant a lot to me too!" I put my hands on my hips. "You're not going to join without me, are you?"

Caroline didn't answer.

"*Are* you?" I asked again.

"I don't see why we have to do *everything* together," she finally blurted out.

My jaw dropped.

"*What?*" I cried. "I can't believe you! You're my best friend. How could you do this to me?"

Caroline raised her head and finally stared me in the eye. "I'm not *doing* anything to you. I'm joining a club."

"Yes. The club we were *both* supposed to be in. And you're joining without me!" My voice became louder and louder. But I couldn't stop it.

"Can I help it if my mom would let me have only four friends to my birthday party? How could I know

5

that Arden would get so upset that I didn't invite her?" I demanded.

Caroline glanced nervously over her shoulder. Arden and her group of Waynesbridge Scouts stared at us. "Keep your voice down, Lizzy. You're embarrassing me."

"So what if you're embarrassed!" I was practically yelling now. "What about me? I've just been labeled a loser! And you don't even care!"

Caroline didn't answer me. She just stood there.

I knew I had to leave. Fast. Before I *totally* lost it—in front of Arden and the entire middle school. I didn't even bother to close my locker. I took off for the nearest exit.

I opened the door and glanced up. It was a creepy, overcast afternoon. Storm clouds darkened the sky. Fog was rolling in.

I took one last peek over my shoulder at Caroline. She had joined the other scouts in the hallway. Arden said something to her. The two of them laughed together.

My face turned red with anger.

"I'll show her," I mumbled as I strode off the school grounds. "I'll show them all."

As I turned onto Cedar Drive, thunder rumbled directly over my head. I jumped and started to walk faster.

The closer I got to home, the more upset I became with Caroline. How could she do this to me?

Overhead, the sky darkened even more. A bolt of

lightning zigzagged through it. A second later, thunder boomed.

Yikes! That seemed really close! I pulled my denim jacket tight around me. The fog grew thicker, heavier.

I want to be home, I thought. Safe in my own room. Away from Waynesbridge Middle School. And Caroline. And this storm.

I ducked my head and was about to make a run for it.

Then someone jumped out at me.

Someone hiding behind a tree.

Someone dressed in black. With a black hood on.

He headed straight for me! My breath caught in my throat.

Who was he?

What did he want?

2

Make that—what did *she* want?

As the figure came toward me, she pushed back the black hood. Long, dark hair spilled out.

It was a girl. A girl about my own age. She was taller than me, with ivory skin and huge, dark brown eyes.

"Hello," she said in a cheery voice. "I'm Amy."

"I—I'm Lizzy," I stammered, catching my breath. "You surprised me, jumping out like that."

Amy smiled. "Sorry."

I waited for her to say something else, but she just kept staring at me.

Weird, I thought. I tried to walk around her. But she stepped sideways, blocking my way again.

8

"I just moved here from Shadyside," Amy finally told me. "I go to Waynesbridge Middle School now."

"Really?" I studied her face. "I've never seen you there."

"We're in different classes," Amy explained. "Anyway, I heard you talking to your friend in the hall at school."

"Ex-friend," I corrected Amy. I could feel my face turn red again. Everybody in the whole school must have heard my fight with Caroline!

Who cares? I decided. Now they all know how mean she was!

"You shouldn't worry about being in the Waynesbridge Scouts," Amy continued. "They seem like a big bunch of snobs."

I shrugged. "I guess they are."

"Why don't you join my troop instead?" Amy suggested.

"Your troop?" I asked.

"It's in Shadyside—the Camp Fear Girls. Have you heard of us?"

I shook my head. "No. But I've heard of Fear *Street*. There are lots of scary stories about it. Ghosts in the cemetery, monsters in the lake. Everyone says it's totally creepy. Some kids at school sort of believe those stories. They never go anywhere near it."

"Well, our group is named after Fear Street. That's why it's so great. We do scary, fun stuff all the time!" Amy leaned in toward me. She practically whispered now. "I know you'd like it. Why don't you come to one meeting?"

"Well . . . " I bit my lip. I didn't know anything about this club. Or anyone in it. But it *did* sound like fun! More fun than the girly Waynesbridge Scouts.

Should I join?

"We're looking for a new member," Amy added. "You'd be *perfect.*"

I shivered. The wind blew cold around me.

Maybe I should talk to Caroline about this, I thought.

Then I remembered. Caroline was a Waynesbridge Scout now. If she could join the scouts without me, then I could join the Camp Fear Girls without her!

"Sure," I said loudly. "I'll join. Sign me up!"

Another bolt of lightning crackled across the sky.

"Great!" Amy cried. "The Camp Fear Girls will be in touch!"

Before I could ask *how* they'd be in touch, Amy disappeared into the fog.

I wanted to run after her. But the fog seemed to swallow her up. She completely vanished!

I turned and ran the rest of the way home. I made it inside my house just as it started raining.

When I raced through the door, Mom shouted her usual greeting from the living room. "Hi! Hang up your coat. And don't dump your books on the floor. Take them to your room."

I muttered back my usual reply. "Okay. Okay."

"Oh, and, Lizzy," Mom added. "You have mail. It's on the kitchen table."

Mail? My relatives send me cards on my birthday, but the rest of the time I don't get any mail.

I sorted through the catalogues and bills stacked on the table. Sure enough, at the bottom of the pile sat an envelope. It had my name—Elizabeth Caldwell—written on it.

Who could it be from?

I tore it open. Inside was an official invitation to join the Camp Fear Girls.

"Whoa!" I murmured. "That was fast! How did they do that?"

Maybe they sent the invitation a while ago, I reasoned. Before Amy invited me in person.

I studied the invitation. Drawings of bats and spiderwebs decorated the edges of the page. A skeleton posed at the top. "Cool," I whispered.

The drawings made me think of scary stories around a campfire. Awesome! This creepy invitation was *much* better than the stupid pink stationery the Waynesbridge Scouts used.

I read the rest of the invitation. It said a van would arrive at my house and take me to the Camp Fear Girls' meeting place. Number 333. On a secret street. The meeting would begin at eight o'clock—tonight.

"Ooh, a secret meeting place." I giggled. I could tell, this was definitely my kind of group!

There was no signature on the bottom of the

invitation. I flipped the paper over. Nothing on the other side either.

I glanced over the letter again. And before my eyes, a new message appeared along the bottom of the page.

"Wow!" I cried as the words magically formed.

Oh, no. It was a warning.

Spelled out in big, red dripping letters.

"BE THERE . . . OR BEWARE!"

3

BE THERE . . . OR BEWARE—it was so creepy!
And *so* cool! I couldn't wait to ask Amy how the
Camp Fear Girls did that. It must be some kind of
disappearing ink.

I ran into the living room to ask my mom if I could
go to the meeting.

It took some serious pleading. Mom didn't see why
I had to pick a club in Shadyside instead of Waynesbridge. And she wanted me to tell her who the other
girls in the troop were. I didn't know. But finally she
agreed. Mostly because *she* didn't have to drive me
there!

A little before eight I stood at our living room
window, peering out at the street. Waiting to go to my
first Camp Fear Girls' meeting.

"What time did you say the van was supposed to pick you up?" Mom called from the kitchen.

"Just before eight," I answered. I checked my watch: 7:55.

"Let me know when the van gets here. I want to meet the driver," Mom told me.

The glare of headlights flashed across our front window. A large black van pulled into our driveway.

"Mom! They're here!" I shouted, grabbing my denim jacket.

Mom walked me out to the van. A gray-haired lady with wire-rimmed glasses sat behind the wheel. When she saw my mother, she smiled.

"I'm Kate Caldwell," Mom introduced herself. "And this is my daughter, Lizzy."

"Pleased to meet you," the older lady replied.

While Mom chatted with the woman, I paced. I couldn't wait to get to the meeting. And it was getting closer and closer to eight o'clock!

"All right," Mom finally said to the driver. "I'll expect to see Lizzy back here by ten o'clock."

"Don't worry about a thing, Mrs. Caldwell," the woman assured Mom. "We'll take good care of your Lizzy."

Mom opened the van's sliding door. I hopped into the back.

"Have fun!" Mom called.

"I will," I told her.

Mom slid the door shut. She stood in the driveway until the van pulled away.

After we traveled about half a block, I leaned forward to speak to the driver.

"So—are you the leader of the Camp Fear Girls?" I asked.

The driver didn't say a word. She clutched the wheel of the van and stared at the road.

Hmmmm, I thought. Maybe I didn't speak loud enough.

I cleared my throat and cupped my hands around my mouth. "I was wondering if you were the scout leader," I shouted.

Silence.

Boy, I thought, she must *really* be deaf.

I tried a different approach. I tapped her on the shoulder. "Excuse me!" I bellowed. "Are you the scout leader?"

The driver didn't even turn to look at me.

This is *weird,* I thought, leaning back in my seat. The driver seemed so friendly before. Now she won't even look at me.

I studied her face in the rearview mirror. Her expression was hard and cold. Like stone.

As we drove along River Road, I kept expecting to stop at one of the houses to pick up Amy or another Camp Fear Girl. But we didn't. I was the only passenger in the black van.

Soon we left the houses and lights of Waynesbridge behind us. Outside, I could just make out the twisted shapes of the trees lining the river.

I stared into the darkness. I didn't know where I was.

My heart began to pound.

How much did I know about this driver? She could be taking me anywhere!

The driver made a sharp right turn. It threw me across the seat. I smashed into the side of the van.

We bumped across Mill Bridge. Good! I knew Mill Bridge. Once we crossed it, we'd be in Shadyside. Not far from the Camp Fear Girls' meeting. I could jump out of the car if I had to.

The van screeched to a halt in the middle of the bridge. The driver turned her head. "This is where you get out," she told me.

I peered into the murky night. Not a soul anywhere. Not a light to guide me. "Excuse me? Did you say I had to get out now?" I asked.

The driver nodded. The van door slid open and a rush of cold, damp air swirled in.

"Wh-why?" I stammered.

"You have to walk the rest of the way." She pointed one gnarled finger into the darkness. "Just follow that street."

I stepped out the open door of the van. I gasped when I read the sign above my head: FEAR STREET!

4

Fear Street! I couldn't believe it! They wanted me to walk down there?

At night?

Alone?

I took one step away from the van. It sped off with its tires squealing.

I glanced nervously down Fear Street. Big old houses lined either side. Trees stretched their strange, twisted limbs across the sky.

All the stories I heard about Fear Street didn't prepare me for how scary it really looked. I stood frozen, afraid to move.

Only one street lamp glowed in the distance. The rest—either burnt out or broken.

"I don't like this," I said to myself in a tiny voice. "I don't like it one bit."

Why would the Camp Fear Girls want me to walk down Fear Street by myself?

"Maybe it's some kind of initiation," I reasoned. "It *is* a creepy club. Maybe they need to make sure I'm not a chicken."

Yeah. That had to be it.

I forced myself to glance ahead. "I'm not afraid," I declared, tilting my chin up. "If the Camp Fear Girls want to see brave—I'll show them brave."

My heart thunked against my rib cage. But I marched down Fear Street with big strides. I swung my arms. I even whistled.

Shadows on the sidewalk seemed to shift and change under my feet. I passed one darkened house after another, looking for the address on the invitation. I muttered, "333," squinting at the numbers on the decaying houses. I didn't see it.

A shutter banged somewhere nearby. I jumped in surprise.

Just a shutter, I told myself. Calm down.

I tried to whistle some more, but I couldn't. My breath was too shaky. So I sang:

> "There was a farmer had a dog,
> And Bingo was his name-oh."

Out of the corner of my eye I spied something darting

from one yard into another. "A cat. Only a cat," I said out loud.

My voice was quivering. I moved more slowly. But I continued singing to the Bingo tune. "Where is 333? Where is 333? Where is 333? I'm getting pretty scared-oh."

Suddenly, all around me, the wind picked up with a giant *whoosh!*

A tree limb slapped at the sides of a wooden house. Up and down the street, gates banged back and forth. Trash cans clattered across front yards.

Another gust blew my hair across my face and into my eyes. The wind felt strangely cold. Wintry. Even though it was spring.

Then I felt the wind pushing at my back. Shoving me. Like invisible hands, guiding me—

Down Fear Street.

"Stop!" I cried. But the more I fought against the wind, the more it pushed me.

I stumbled forward, past house after house. Farther and farther down the awful, dark street.

I clutched at a rickety fence and held on tight. The wind whipped around my hands. It pried my fingers off the wooden post, one by one.

Then it continued to shove me down the street.

I clawed at the hair in front of my face, trying to see what lay ahead.

I could just make out a brick wall and big iron bars.

A gate! With letters arched across the top of it.

I squinted, struggling to read it.

"No!" I shrieked when I finally read the words. "Not in there! Please don't make me go in there!"

5

"Nooo!" I yelled at the top of my lungs. Not the Fear Street Cemetery!

As if it heard me, the wind stopped. Just like that. And the night was quiet again.

I stood there for a moment while my heartbeat slowed down.

What *was* that wind? Where did it come from? Where did it go? Could I have imagined the way it shoved me?

Of course I imagined it.

Fear Street had given me the creeps. That's all.

I pushed my hair out of my eyes and gazed around.

I stood a few yards to the side of the cemetery gate. One rickety old house stood directly in front of me. It had lots of carved wooden decorations around the porch. From the walkway I could see the huge spider-webs that hung off them.

The front steps were splintered and sagging. The screen on the front door hung open on one twisted hinge. The weeds sprouting from the lawn were nearly as tall as me.

I read the address out loud: "333."

I thought the invitation said 333. But that couldn't be right.

I thought we would be meeting at one of the members' houses. But no one could possibly live here. This place was a wreck!

I dug into the pocket of my jacket and pulled out my invitation. Even in the dim light, it was easy to read the big bold numbers: *333*.

Yes. This was definitely the right address.

"Weird," I murmured, making my way up the broken steps.

Creak!

A board bent under my foot. It began to splinter and crack. I jumped forward.

CRRRACK! The board snapped in half.

Whoa! This is dangerous, I realized. My foot could have gone right through!

I stepped carefully over to a nearby window and peered inside. I couldn't see anything. The glass was caked with dust and cobwebs, inside and out.

Then I moved to the door. I knocked gently.

Tap. Tap. Tap.

Strange laughter floated from inside the old house.

It sounded warped. Slowed down. Like a tape recorder with its batteries running low.

I shivered. Who—or what—could laugh like that?

I froze, listening. I couldn't hear anyone coming to the door.

I took a shaky breath. I slowly reached out and rapped on the door again. This time harder.

Ha-ha-ha-ha-ha.

I shuddered. That creepy laughter again! And still no one came to the door.

Something was wrong here. Very wrong.

I *had* to be in the wrong place.

"I'm out of here," I declared loudly. "Who needs the Camp—"

My words died in my throat. An icy cold hand gripped my shoulder!

6

I spun around. And saw Amy!

"You scared me!" I gasped.

"That was the idea," Amy told me, wiggling her eyebrows.

She was dressed in a dark blue pleated skirt and white blouse with a red bandanna around her neck. A matching red sash with several rows of badges sewn to it hung across her chest.

"Why are you standing out here?" Amy asked. "Wouldn't they let you in?"

I shook my head. "I wasn't sure I was in the right place. I could hear people laughing inside, but nobody answered when I knocked."

Amy slapped her forehead with the palm of her

hand. "Oh, that's right. You don't know the secret knock."

She crossed to the door and tapped three times, slowly. Then two times fast, and then three more times slowly.

The front door creaked open.

"See?" Amy shrugged. "Nothing to it."

I followed Amy through the darkened entry. I turned to see who opened the door.

There was no one there! Did the door open all by itself?

No. That was dumb. The door had probably been unlatched all this time. When Amy knocked, it swung open. That's all.

Amy led me into a room to the right of the front door. It was brightly lit—and filled with all sorts of cool stuff. A big-screen TV took up one wall. Next to it I saw a VCR, a five-CD player, a Sega, *and* a Super Nintendo game system and two speaker towers. Big leather couches circled a snack table that was piled high with chips, soda, and cookies.

"Awesome!" I whispered to myself. The inside of this house was nothing like the outside.

Four girls in uniforms like Amy's knelt by the snack table, eating. Three others stood by the entertainment system. Three more sat on the couch. One stood by the windows.

I did a quick count in my head. Eleven girls. And Amy made twelve. Twelve new friends.

"Attention, everybody," Amy called. "This is Lizzy. She's our new recruit."

All eleven girls turned their heads at the exact same moment. "Hi, Lizzy," they called.

Amy walked me around the room, introducing me. There was a red-haired girl named Trudy, and a tall, thin girl named Violet. Priscilla had dark frizzy hair. Lorraine's was short and blond.

Pearl, a pretty girl with two long brown braids, stood by the window. All the girls wore red sashes across their uniforms, like Amy. All except Pearl. Hers was purple. Maybe that means she's some kind of troop leader, I guessed.

"Pearl, this is Lizzy," Amy said, introducing me. "She's from Waynesbridge."

Pearl smiled and stuck out her hand. "Cool. Welcome to my house, Lizzy. And welcome to the troop."

"Thanks," I replied, clasping her hand.

"Um, where's your scout leader?" I asked, gazing around the room and back toward the front door.

"Oh, that would be Pearl's mother. She had to run some errands," Amy explained. "But she left us lots of snacks. Have some, Lizzy."

"Thanks," I said, eyeing the tortilla chips.

While I munched on some chips, Amy, Trudy, and Pearl took thick green candles from a cupboard. They passed them out to the rest of the Camp Fear Girls, who lit them.

Then Trudy flicked out the ceiling light. Pearl moved to the front of our group.

"Didn't I promise you some scary fun?" Amy whispered, sitting next to me. "It's story time!"

I took a quick peek around the room. The green candles must have come from a special horror shop or something. Their light made everyone look spooky.

Cool, I thought. This was going to be great! Scary stories in a house on Fear Street!

I turned my attention back to Pearl, who was starting her story.

"Since Lizzy is new here, I will tell the story of the first troop of Camp Fear Girls." Pearl leaned forward and spoke in an eerie voice. "This story begins almost one hundred years ago. Thirteen girls—a troop of Shadyside scouts called the Camp Fear Girls—decided to go for a camp-out in the Fear Street Woods. Those thirteen girls left home and were never seen again.

"Their families searched and searched for these thirteen girls, but they were never found."

Pearl raised her candle to just below her chin.

"There are rumors—wild, horrible rumors," she continued, "that those thirteen scouts were turned into hideous monsters. By who—or what—no one knows."

As Pearl spoke, the candle cast strange shadows on the wall.

One shadow, behind Pearl, seemed larger than the others. I fixed my eyes on it. The shadow seemed to have a head. And sharp teeth. And claws!

A monster!

I blinked. The shadow was just a black blob again.

Wow! I was totally freaking myself out. Pearl's story was really creepy!

Pearl lowered her voice to a hoarse whisper. "Those monsters still roam Shadyside today, looking for new people to add to their troop.

"And once you join, you can never leave. You become one of the undead. Your body becomes like theirs. Your skin rots and falls off your bones. Your eyes sink back into your head. And you are forced to walk the earth that way—forever!"

My eyes went wide with horror.

I felt Amy tap me on the shoulder. "Pretty scary, huh, Lizzy?" she whispered in my ear.

I turned around to agree with her—and screamed!

Amy's skin was grayish-green.

One eye dangled—out of its socket.

A huge open cut ran down the side of her face. Green slime oozed from it.

Amy was a monster!

7

I screamed until my throat burned with pain.

I jumped up. I backed away from the hideous thing in front of me.

Amy, the monster, staggered to her feet. Her mouth was fixed in an evil leer. She stepped toward me. Slobber dripped from her mouth.

"No! Get away from me!" I screamed.

I ran to the door. But as I reached it, it slammed shut!

I lunged for the doorknob. Pulled at it with all my might.

It wouldn't budge!

I whirled around. Amy moved closer and closer. I pressed my back against the door.

29

She bent her horrible face toward mine. I raised my arms to protect myself.

"Get away!" I pleaded. "Get away!"

Slowly, Amy lifted her right hand. Reaching for me.

"Nooo!" I wailed.

Then she brushed her hand over her chin—her face began to peel off!

I screamed and shut my eyes. I couldn't bear to watch!

"Gotcha!" Amy shouted.

I opened one eye.

Amy was back to normal. A hideous rubber mask hung limply in her hand.

My other eye flew open. I couldn't believe it! The whole thing was a joke!

Amy laughed so hard, tears rolled down her cheeks. The other girls were laughing too.

Amy held up the rubber monster mask for everyone to see. Then she swatted my shoulder with it. She gasped out big, hiccupy laughs.

My cheeks grew hot. My whole face felt on fire.

I couldn't believe I fell for their joke.

Pearl was laughing the hardest. She set down her candle and bent over, clutching her stomach.

"That was part of your initiation," she managed to choke out. "And you passed!"

Huh? I blinked. I turned to look at Amy. "I passed?"

Amy was still giggling so hard, she couldn't talk. She nodded her head.

If screaming your head off meant you passed, what did you have to do to fail?

I glanced around the room. All of the other girls gave me big welcoming smiles.

"Great. I'm so glad I passed," I muttered.

Pearl held up one finger. "One down," she announced.

"What do you mean, 'one down'?" I asked.

"You passed the first test," Trudy explained. "But there's another one."

"To become a full-fledged member of our troop, you'll have to go on the overnight camp-out," Pearl said.

I love camp-outs. But would they pull more jokes like this one?

"Okay," I said, trying to sound enthusiastic. "I guess you can count me in."

"Good!" Amy patted me on the back.

Violet showed me a notebook that had the words CAMP FEAR GIRLS GUIDEBOOK, embossed in gold letters on the navy blue cover.

She sat cross-legged next to Pearl and declared, "On our camp-out, Lizzy, you'll earn your first three badges."

I glanced across the room at Pearl's sash. She had lots of badges sewn on it. In really cool colors.

I started getting excited. I'd love to earn some of those badges, I thought, and show them off to Caroline.

31

"Can I really earn all three badges in one night?" I asked.

Amy waved one hand. "Don't worry. It's easy."

She pointed to the badges on her own sash. One had an artist's brush and palette embroidered on it. "This is the arts and crafts badge," she explained.

Trudy pointed to the badge beside it. It was also embroidered, but with a picture of a gray rock. "That's the rock-collecting badge."

Another badge showed a girl swimming freestyle in a lake. "And that's the swimming badge," Violet concluded. "Piece of cake."

I had to admit, they all seemed easy enough to earn. I smiled with relief.

Until I caught a glimpse of Amy's other badges!

8

"**A** coffin!" I pointed at the badge under Amy's swimming patch. "That badge has a picture of a coffin on it! And *that* one looks like a knife." I poked at the next badge with my finger.

A slow smile crept across Amy's lips. She wiggled her eyebrows. "Awesome, isn't it?"

The next badge was a rope. Was it for knot-tying? But then, why was the rope shaped like a hangman's noose?

"What's *that* for?" I asked.

"Fun!" Pearl gestured to the badges on her purple sash. "They're all for fun."

"It's much more fun to earn these than stupid old cooking badges," Amy explained. "Or a wimpy *gardening* badge like the Waynesbridge Scouts earn."

"Aren't our badges totally scary?" Violet giggled. "They're perfect for our club."

"Look, Lizzy. We thought you were someone who liked a good scare. You're not *afraid* of some silly badges, are you?" Trudy asked, sticking her face in front of mine.

"Of course not," I shot back.

"Are you *sure?*" Pearl demanded. "Because we don't want any babies in this troop." She narrowed her eyes at me suspiciously. "Hey, how old *are* you anyway?"

That made me mad. Maybe I *was* the shortest kid in the seventh grade. So what? What difference did that make?

"I'm old enough to go on a camp-out," I snapped. "And I'm old enough to earn those badges."

A grin spread across Pearl's face. "All right. You're in," she declared. She stuck her hand into the center of the circle. The others piled their hands on top of hers. "Welcome to the Camp Fear Girls," Pearl sang out.

"Welcome!" the girls repeated.

I placed my hand on top of the stack.

A freezing breeze drifted through the room.

Brrr! What a drafty old house, I thought.

"Pearl!" Trudy called when we broke our handhold. "Did you forget that tonight is Prank Night?"

Several of the girls squealed with delight.

"Prank Night is a troop favorite," Amy whispered to me.

34

"How could I forget?" Pearl grinned. "I *live* for Prank Night."

"Yeah!" "Me too!" the others agreed.

Pearl raised one hand and the group fell silent. Then she asked in a spooky voice, "Who should we play our prank on tonight?"

Several girls raised their hands to make suggestions, but Amy cupped her hands around her mouth and shouted, "Since Lizzy is going to be our newest member, let's let her choose."

"Brilliant idea." Pearl turned to me. "Well? Who would you really like to *get?*"

I stared into Pearl's eyes. They reflected the yellow flicker of the candlelight. And suddenly a strange feeling crept through me. A wild feeling I couldn't explain.

I tried to break my gaze, but Pearl's eyes held mine. The yellow candle flicker seemed to grow into a burning glow.

My eyes narrowed to little slits, and a wicked smile curled the corners of my lips.

And then, as if someone were controlling my thoughts, I whispered, "Caroline. Let's get Caroline!"

9

"**C**aroline is Lizzy's ex-friend," Amy told the troop.

Pearl raised her eyebrows. "*Ex*-friend? *Ex*cellent!"

Amy rubbed her hands together. "Let's send her a message—with slime!"

She led everyone into the kitchen. Big metal buckets sat on the counter. They were filled with a white, pasty goo.

"What's in there?" I whispered to Amy.

"Flour, cornstarch, and water. Now we're going to mix in this green food coloring," Amy said, holding up a bottle. She poured the green dye into the bucket.

"Don't forget the secret slime ingredient!" Trudy shouted. She rushed over and dropped some powder into the bucket. The muck inside began to bubble and fizz.

"Wow! What is that stuff?" I asked.

Pearl pressed a wooden spatula into my hand. "Just trust us. Stir this up, and we'll give your friend Caroline—"

"My *ex*-friend," I corrected her.

"—your *ex*-friend Caroline a big surprise," she finished.

I dipped the spoon into the sticky goop and stirred it hard. The more I stirred, the more it bubbled and hissed. And it smelled *awful*. Like a skunk dipped in vinegar.

Evil thoughts of pouring that green gunk all over Caroline's head flashed through my mind.

I stopped in mid-stir. Whoa! I never had a thought that mean in my life. Where did it come from?

Pearl patted me on the shoulder. "Keep stirring," she instructed. "When it's done, we'll go over to Caroline's and give her a little present."

"We'll send her a message," Trudy added as she stirred her own bucket. "One she'll never forget."

That evil feeling washed over me again. I'd write something rotten on Caroline's porch with the slime. And then I'd run! It would take forever to get that green dye off the porch, I thought. Good!

Priscilla and Violet had been working on their bucket of slime across the kitchen. "We've got goop!" they called.

"All right, everybody," Pearl announced. "Let's head 'em up and move 'em out."

There were three buckets of slime in all. Amy and I

37

carried ours between us as the troop marched down Fear Street.

"Caroline lives on Pine Ridge Road," I told them. "About two blocks from my house."

We crossed Mill Bridge and slipped silently through Waynesbridge. We took side streets so no one would see us.

Caroline's two-story gray-and-white house sat in the middle of the block. Light glowed from the kitchen in back and the upstairs bedroom windows. I knew Caroline was home.

"When we reach the house," Amy whispered, "you go up to the porch. We'll be right behind you."

I nodded, and gave Amy a thumbs-up.

My heart thumped with excitement. In a few seconds Caroline would get her slimy message—and I would have my revenge.

We reached the lawn. Carrying my bucket, I led the way to the front porch. The troop followed.

That dark, evil feeling grew inside me again. I could feel it clouding my brain. Taking over. All I could think was "Get Caroline. Get her!"

I knelt on the porch. I spooned out a glop of the bubbling slime. What should I write? I wanted to find the perfect nasty words that would make Caroline feel truly awful!

Trudy marched past me to the front door.

"Wait!" I whispered. "What are you doing?"

Without answering me, Trudy pressed the doorbell.

I scrambled to my feet. "Are you nuts? Caroline's dad will come to the door. We'll get caught!"

All at once the troop scattered. Several of the girls hid in the bushes. Amy ducked behind Caroline's dad's car.

I barely had enough time to dive into the shadow of a weeping willow tree.

The front door creaked open. I peeked out from under the trailing branches. Someone stood in the doorway.

From my hiding place I couldn't see the person's face. But I could make out a navy blue T-shirt.

Caroline!

She took two steps onto the dark porch. Probably searching for whoever rang the bell.

What's going on? I wondered. What are the Camp Fear Girls planning?

Suddenly, I saw movement in the bushes. The whole troop stood up in their hiding places.

Trudy raised her head above the hedge. Pearl stood by the porch, her purple sash catching the light from inside the house.

Amy stepped silently from behind the car. She held a bucket in her hands.

All at once it hit me.

They weren't going to write a message. They really *were* going to dump their buckets of bubbling ooze on Caroline! Just the way I had imagined it!

The dark feeling inside my brain totally cleared.

They can't do that, I thought. What if the bubbling ooze does something horrible to her? I don't want to *hurt* her.

I leaped out from my hiding place to cry, "Stop!"

But before I could say it—

Splat!

10

Slime flew through the air from three different directions. It hit Caroline dead-on.

Green goo dripped from her head. Her arms. Her favorite blue T-shirt.

I was glad I couldn't see her face. I knew she must be furious. And scared.

"Run!" Amy yelled.

I pounded away from Caroline's house as fast as my feet would carry me. The rest of the Camp Fear Girls were right behind me. They laughed loudly as they ran.

I put my head down and pumped my legs furiously. I had to get away fast—before Caroline saw me! If she did, she'd never, ever speak to me again!

We clattered across Mill Bridge. When I glanced up again, we were back at the house on Fear Street.

I climbed the rickety porch stairs. Then I bent over to catch my breath.

I felt terrible. That prank was supposed to be fun, but it wasn't. I felt like a total jerk.

I wanted to say something about it. To tell the girls I didn't really like Prank Night—and I never wanted to do it again. But Pearl didn't give me the chance.

"Hurry and join the troop in the living room," Pearl ordered, adjusting her purple sash. "It's time to bring tonight's meeting to a close."

The twelve girls waited in a circle, in silence. They clasped each other's hands.

Then Pearl started to sing in a low, spooky voice.

"Thirteen girls went off to camp.
The woods were dark, the ground was damp."

The other girls joined in.

"Thirteen families dressed in black.
Thirteen girls who never came back."

The hair on the back of my neck stood up. They were singing about that camp-out a hundred years ago! Creepy! They ended the song with a warning.

"So if you camp in the Fear Street Woods,
Thirteen girls will get you good!"

Finally, everyone unclasped their hands. And the meeting was over.

I sighed with relief.

What a totally weird experience!

Amy didn't walk with me back toward Waynesbridge. She said she was spending the night in Shadyside—at Trudy's. I had to go back down Fear Street by myself again. At ten o'clock at night.

I reached the bridge in record time. I began to jog across it—and was suddenly blinded by headlights.

The van! It stopped right in front of me. The same weird lady sat behind the wheel.

She didn't look at me. But she gestured with her thumb to the backseat. "Get in," she ordered.

I hesitated.

"Didn't you hear me?" the old woman barked. "I said, get in."

I climbed into the backseat and slid the door shut. We rumbled across Mill Bridge.

I didn't even try to talk to the driver this time. I just wanted to go home and get into bed. I needed time to think about the Camp Fear Girls.

After what happened, I wasn't so sure I wanted to be a part of their troop anymore. Sure, I liked scary things. But maybe these girls were *too* scary. Too weird. Too *mean.*

When the van dropped me in front of my house, I leaped out and raced inside. Home!

My parents sat on the couch, watching the late

news in the living room. They watched me turn the dead bolt and slip the chain lock in place.

Dad raised his eyebrows. "Locking the monsters out for the night, Lizzy?" he asked.

"Uh—yeah. You could say that," I answered.

"How was the meeting?" Mom asked.

"Fine," I mumbled, hanging up my jean jacket.

Mom frowned. "You don't sound very enthusiastic."

"I'm a little tired," I replied, heading straight for the stairs.

I didn't want to talk about the meeting with them. I was afraid I might blab and tell them all about Prank Night. Then I'd get in big trouble.

I was halfway upstairs when Dad yelled, "Oh, Lizzy, I almost forgot. Caroline called. She said it was really important you call her back."

I felt as though someone punched me in the stomach.

"Caroline?" I repeated in a shaky voice.

"She said to call no matter how late you got in."

"Oh, no!" I whispered. My hand gripped the stair railing.

She *knows.*

Caroline was slimed . . . and *she knows I did it.*

I stared at the phone in my parents' bedroom.

I have to call Caroline, I thought. I have to say I'm sorry. Or at least try to explain.

I put my hand on the receiver. "Here goes."

I didn't even have to think about the number. My fingers knew it by heart: 555-4239.

One ring. My stomach did somersaults as I waited for someone to pick up.

Two rings.

Come on, Caroline. Let me get this over with!

"Hurt residence, Caroline speaking."

It's her. Now what do I do? I thought.

"Hello?" Caroline sounded irritated. "Hel-loooooh."

It was now or never.

I spoke really fast. "Caroline-it's-me-Lizzy."

"Lizzy!" Caroline yelled.

I winced. *Oh, no. Here it comes.*

But instead of screaming at me, Caroline burst out laughing. "You will not *believe* what just happened at my house."

I frowned. Why was she laughing?

"I had to call you right away," Caroline continued. "My brother, Chip, just got . . . oh, it's too funny to even say." She laughed some more before she could finish her sentence. "Lizzy, Chip just got *slimed!*"

"Chip got slimed?" I asked. "Your brother Chip?"

"Yes! Oh, Lizzy, you should have seen him. He was covered from head to toe in this disgusting green goop." Caroline laughed so hard, she snorted. And that made her laugh even harder.

I stood there holding the phone. *Chip?*

He must have been wearing a shirt the same color as Caroline's. And they *were* about the same height. And, after all, I had never gotten a look at the person's face. . . .

I collapsed on my parents' bed. Whew! That was close!

I started to giggle along with Caroline. Half from relief. And half from hearing her snort. It felt really good to be talking to her again.

"And boy, did he stink!" she exclaimed when she could speak again. "I don't know what was in that stuff, but—"

"Listen, Caroline," I cut in. "I'm sorry about how I

yelled at you this afternoon. I'm really glad you got into the Waynesbridge Scouts. I acted like a jerk."

Caroline paused. Then her tone changed completely. She wasn't laughing anymore. "I'm sorry too. You were so upset. And I didn't help you at all. You should have been picked for the scouts too. It wasn't fair."

"Let's not fight anymore," I said earnestly. "You're my best friend. And I want it to stay that way."

"Me too," Caroline agreed. Then she giggled again. "Remember the best-friend cheer we made up in second grade?"

"Yup," I said. I started the cheer.

"We're the very best of friends,
We'll be best friends till the end."

Caroline joined in and together we shouted the end of the cheer: "B-E-S-T, best friends!"

We both laughed. I suddenly felt lighter. Happier. We were friends again!

"So how was your first meeting of the Waynesbridge Scouts?" I finally asked.

"You really want to hear?" Caroline asked.

"Really," I replied. I wasn't faking. I wanted to know.

"Well it was kind of—dull," Caroline admitted. "I guess I wanted to be a scout for so long that I expected it to be a lot more fun."

"What did you do?" I asked.

47

"We sat around on folding chairs in the Sitwells' living room, sipped little cups of tea, and introduced ourselves."

"You're kidding!" I gasped.

"No. Can you believe it? We *introduced* ourselves—like we all haven't known each other since preschool." I could tell by Caroline's tone of voice that she was rolling her eyes.

"Why did you have to introduce yourselves?" I asked.

"Mrs. Sitwell thought we should learn manners. So we each had to stand up and tell a little story about ourselves and our family." Caroline made a snoring sound. "Bor-ing."

"Didn't you play any games?"

"No. Arden passed around cookies with pink icing. We sipped our tea. And then we went home."

I shook my head. "That's amazing. My meeting was the complete opposite."

"Your meeting? What meeting did you go to?"

I forgot that Caroline didn't know about the Camp Fear Girls. So I quickly filled her in on how I ran into Amy on the way home from school. I also told her about the invitation with the weird, drippy letters that suddenly appeared at the bottom of the page. She thought that was cool too.

Then I told her about the rickety old house on Fear Street with the great club room inside. I mentioned the scary stories and the camp-out, but I didn't tell her about Prank Night.

Caroline giggled excitedly. "Scary stories, weird special effects and a camp-out—it sounds awesome."

"It's *totally* awesome," I bluffed. I didn't want to tell Caroline that the Camp Fear Girls *weren't* totally fun. Sometimes they were just plain creepy. I guess I was still hurt about not being in the Waynesbridge Scouts. I couldn't help it—I wanted Caroline to think my troop was better than hers.

"Mrs. Sitwell showed us the badges we would have to earn. Baking and housekeeping and *gardening*. Is that lame or what? I thought this was a cool club, but now it seems completely *un*cool," Caroline admitted.

I thought about the Camp Fear Girls' badges—and shuddered. Maybe baking cookies wasn't all that boring.

But I didn't let on to Caroline. "That *is* lame," I agreed.

"I wish I were in *your* troop," Caroline said wistfully. "You are so lucky. I don't think my troop would ever camp out—unless the campground was called the Holiday Inn."

I giggled. Caroline was right. It was hard to imagine Shannon, or Arden, or any of those Waynesbridge girls hiking anywhere. Let alone sleeping on the ground!

"Hey, Lizzy," Caroline said. "Don't you think it would be way cool if we could both be in the same troop?"

"You mean the Waynesbridge Scouts?" I asked.

"No, forget them. I want to join the Camp Fear Girls!"

Uh-oh. Me and my big mouth. My plan to make Caroline jealous had worked *too* well!

"Do you think they'd let me join? They sound totally wild," Caroline said.

Wild? She didn't know how right she was!

"Uh—gee, Caroline," I stammered. "I don't know—"

"Why not?" Caroline interrupted.

"Well—uh—" What could I say? "Uh—the Camp Fear Girls won't take just anybody. You have to be asked."

"What are you trying to say? That they wouldn't *want* me?"

"No, I didn't mean—it's just—"

Caroline cut me off. "Lizzy, I know what's going on here—you're trying to keep me out on purpose. You're still mad, aren't you? And that's why you won't even try to get me in!"

Oh, boy! I wasn't even sure *I* wanted to be in the Camp Fear Girls anymore. But now I was stuck. If I didn't try to get Caroline into the troop, we'd have another fight. In fact, we were headed for one now.

"Okay," I agreed glumly. "I'll try to get you in."

I decided to take Caroline to meet Pearl. Pearl's mom was the troop leader, after all. And anyway, I didn't know where Amy or the other girls lived.

The next night after dinner, Caroline met me at the

corner. Together we walked across Mill Bridge to Shadyside.

"Fear Street." Caroline read the street sign out loud.

I nodded. "We're going to number 333."

Caroline shivered. "This street is the scariest place in all of Shadyside and Waynesbridge put together. Maybe in the whole world!"

We passed the first house—and heard a strange howl. An animal darted across the lawn and vanished into the darkness.

"Just a cat," I told Caroline, trying to sound confident.

Caroline jerked her head around, checking the yards in front of us and behind us.

Down the street, a shutter thumped rhythmically against the side of a wooden house. *Whump! Whump! Whump!*

How could it be banging like that? I wondered. I didn't feel a breeze.

Caroline grabbed my arm. "How much farther is it?"

"It's just ahead," I told her. I remembered the last meeting, when the wind pushed me toward the Fear Street Cemetery. Right near the gate stood 333.

Caroline squinted at the numbers on the nearest house. "There's 331."

"Good," I said. "That means 333 should be the next one."

But when we got to the next house, it didn't look

familiar to me. Sheets of plywood were nailed across the front door. The front porch had collapsed at one end.

"Is this it?" Caroline asked with a frown.

"No." I pointed to the metal numbers nailed beside the front door. "See? That's 335."

Caroline spun in a circle. "Then where's 333?"

"I'm not sure," I muttered. I took two steps into the street and peered at the numbers on the house across the way. "That's 332. And that other one is 334."

Caroline turned to face the boarded-up house. "So this should be 333."

"But it's not," I said. "The numbers say 335."

"Maybe the numbering is off." Caroline tugged me down the street. "Do any of those houses look familiar?"

I shook my head. None of them did. "There's 337, 339—and then we're at the cemetery."

"So where's 333?" Caroline demanded.

I shook my head, totally baffled. "It's gone," I murmured. "Completely vanished!"

12

Caroline put her hands on her hips. "Stop kidding around, Lizzy. Houses don't just disappear! Now, which house is it, really?"

"It's 333 Fear Street," I insisted. "But it isn't here!"

Caroline's face turned that slight shade of red it gets when she's really mad. "You're doing this on purpose!" she shouted. "You're still mad at me. I bet you made up the Camp Fear Girls just so you could drag me down Fear Street!"

"No, I didn't," I protested. "I was at a meeting in 333 Fear Street just last night."

Caroline rolled her eyes. "Yeah, sure you were."

I raised my right hand. "Caroline, I swear I'm telling the truth."

Caroline stood on the sidewalk, glaring at me. "I don't believe you."

"Fine!" I snapped. "Don't." I retraced my steps down the sidewalk. Maybe 333 Fear Street would magically appear.

It didn't.

"You can't just leave me here," Caroline complained as she raced to join me.

"I'm not leaving you," I shot back. "I'm trying to find that house. I spent a whole evening there. My mom saw the invitation. If you don't believe me, ask her."

Caroline stared down the street at the house with the banging shutter. "Then tell me how the house just disappeared," she whispered. "Explain that."

I ran one hand through my hair. "I can't explain it," I grumbled. "It doesn't make any sense."

The lone street lamp that had been lighting Fear Street suddenly flickered out.

"Oh, no." Caroline clutched my arm and squeaked, "Lizzy, why did that happen?"

"I don't know," I answered stiffly. "But I'm not sticking around to find out."

"Let's get *out of here!*" we shouted together.

Caroline and I nearly tripped over each other's feet running out of Shadyside. I knew I shouldn't have come back to Fear Street. I knew it!

We raced up the street. Ahead of us, Mill Bridge loomed in the darkness. Our feet thumped onto the wooden bridge.

Halfway across, Caroline stopped to catch her breath. "We made it," she breathed. "We . . ."

Her words trailed off. I followed her glance. A figure stepped from the shadows.

I clutched Caroline's arm. Who was coming toward us?

"Lizzy!" a voice called from the darkness.

I blinked.

"A-A-Amy?" I asked in a quavery voice. "Is that you?"

"Uh-huh," Amy answered, joining us.

"What are *you* doing here?" I asked.

"I went to Trudy's after school," Amy told us. "I was just walking home."

"What happened to Pearl's house?" I blurted out.

Amy frowned. "What are you talking about?"

"Pearl's house, 333 Fear Street. It doesn't *exist* anymore! I walked up and down Fear Street a zillion times!" I babbled. "And I couldn't find it! It isn't there!"

"Of course it's there," Amy said, laughing. "You must have missed it, that's all. Get a grip, Lizzy!"

Amy sounded so certain. Could it be? Could I really have missed the house?

Caroline nudged me. "Lizzy, aren't you going to introduce us?" she whispered.

"Oh, yeah. Uh—Caroline, this is Amy," I muttered. "Amy, meet Caroline."

"Caroline?" Amy repeated. She arched one eyebrow.

I gulped. I'd forgotten all about Prank Night!

I rushed on before Amy could mention it in front of Caroline. "See, Caroline was invited to join the Waynesbridge Scouts," I explained. "But she thought they were kind of boring. When I told her about our troop, the Camp Fear Girls, she thought we sounded fun. So I was taking her to meet Pearl."

"You told her about the troop?" Amy asked, looking at Caroline for the first time.

Caroline nodded and flashed a big smile. "Lizzy said she would get me in."

"I'd like Caroline to join our troop," I added. "If that's all right."

Amy's eyes flew wide.

"No way. It's not all right," she declared.

"How come?" I asked, startled. Did she have to sound so rude? "You picked me, and your friends didn't even know me."

"Thirteen," Amy whispered. "There can be only thirteen."

"Huh? What are you talking about?"

"Only thirteen girls. No more," Amy replied, her voice deadly serious.

Caroline turned to me. I could see she was angry. And embarrassed. "What kind of a club is this anyway?" she demanded. "You can't have more than thirteen girls? That's just *too* weird. I'm out of here."

She marched around Amy and strode across the bridge.

"Caroline, wait!" I called after her. But she didn't answer.

"Can't you bend the rules a *little?*" I pleaded with Amy.

Amy backed away from me. Her dark eyes were bigger than ever. She looked almost . . . frightened. "No. We can't change them. Not ever. Thirteen. It has to be thirteen."

Caroline was right. The club rules *were* too weird. I opened my mouth to argue.

Then it hit me.

This was it! This was my way out of the Camp Fear Girls! Now I could quit without seeming like a wimp!

"Listen, Amy," I said. "Either Caroline and I join the Camp Fear Girls together—or I quit!"

Amy jerked backward as if she'd just been punched in the stomach. "You—you mean you won't become our next member if Caroline can't join?" she asked.

I folded my arms across my chest and shook my head.

Amy's scared expression suddenly faded. She grinned.

It was a nasty grin.

"Well," she said. "We can't have you quit, can we?"

Her tone made the hair on the back of my neck stand up.

Amy closed her eyes for a moment. She looked as if she was thinking hard.

I started to say good-bye.

Then a chilling scream ripped through the night air.

57

13

"**W**hat was that?" I cried.

I raced to the side of the bridge and peered over. It seemed as if the scream came from underneath. Was someone there? I couldn't tell. Everything was pitch black.

"Amy, didn't you hear that scream?" I cried.

Amy didn't reply. Or move.

"Didn't you hear that scream?" I demanded again.

"What scream?" A girl's voice floated up from beneath the bridge. "I didn't hear a scream. Did you?"

"Don't be ridiculous," another voice said from below. "No one screamed."

The voices sounded familiar. I ran around the end

of the bridge. Then I scrambled down the steep bank to the river.

Shadowy figures moved toward me. I felt my throat tighten.

Then one of them stepped into the pool of light from the bridge lamp.

It was Trudy!

In fact, now I could see that *all* the Camp Fear Girls were there. They stood in a group, facing me.

"What are you guys doing under the bridge?" I asked.

Trudy gestured to a pile of discarded soda cans and shredded cardboard. "We're cleaning up the Conononka River. We told you about it last night, remember?"

"It's for our Save the Earth badges," Violet explained.

What? I was totally confused.

"Didn't *any* of you hear that scream?" I asked.

Trudy shrugged. "You hear lots of weird sounds when you're by the river. It was probably a wild animal."

I frowned. That scream did *not* sound like it came from an animal. It sounded like a girl.

I watched as Trudy tossed the pile of litter into a big plastic bag. The others joined in.

Everything seemed perfectly normal. If something awful had happened, the Camp Fear Girls sure weren't acting like it.

"Lizzy, could you hand me that cardboard box by your feet?" Priscilla called. "It looks soggy, so be careful."

"Okay," I replied. I picked up the box and dropped it into the sack. Then I glanced around the group.

Everyone seemed perfectly fine.

But something was different. Someone was missing.

Who?

I wove my way through the group, taking in everyone's faces.

"Pearl!" I announced. "Pearl's missing."

No one answered. No one even looked at me.

I tapped Amy on the shoulder. "Where's Pearl?"

"Our troop agreed to clean up all the areas under Shadyside's bridges," Amy said.

Huh? She totally ignored my question!

"That's great. Where's Pearl?" I asked again.

"Okay, that does it, troop," Trudy announced. "Let's head 'em up and move 'em out."

Wait! Why won't anyone answer me? I wanted to yell. But I didn't. What was going on? I felt so confused!

Could something be wrong with *me?* I wondered. Had I really missed an entire house? Had I forgotten some announcement about tonight's meeting? Was I hearing things—like screams?

I shook my head, trying to clear out my brain. I turned for one last look at the river. In the moonlight the river looked like swirling black oil.

Then I caught a glimpse of something on the water. Something made of purple cloth.

"Oh, no." I let out a low groan.

Pearl's purple sash!

"Guys," I called. "Look!"

But there was no one there.

The Camp Fear Girls had vanished!

14

Oh, no! The Camp Fear Girls had all gone home! I was alone!

I turned back to the water. Frantically, I scanned for the purple sash.

It was gone too.

I stared hard at the inky water. Was Pearl in there somewhere?

But the river flowed smoothly under the bridge. Nothing broke its dark surface.

Maybe I *didn't* see the sash, I thought as I climbed back up to Mill Bridge. Maybe I imagined it because I was already so freaked out.

That was it, I decided. I had just imagined it. Fear Street had made me nervous. The Camp Fear Girls had made me nervous. Maybe I wasn't really as into scary stuff as I thought. Because the Camp Fear Girls were just too creepy for me.

Oh, well. At least it was all over now. The Camp Fear Girls wouldn't let Caroline join. And I wouldn't join without her. So I was out. End of story.

I should have known it wouldn't be that easy.

The phone was ringing when I walked in the front door. Probably Caroline, calling to yell at me about the Camp Fear Girls.

"Lizzy, it's me!" Caroline cried into the phone. "You'll never guess what I got!"

Caroline didn't sound mad. That was a relief.

"What?" I asked, reaching for an apple on the table.

"An invitation from the Camp Fear Girls. They want me to go on their camp-out."

I nearly choked on my apple. "What? Are you sure it's an invitation?"

"Positive," Caroline replied. "It's very official looking. There's even a permission slip for my parents to sign."

Huh? Amy just said Caroline couldn't join.

How come there was room for her all of a sudden?

And another thing. How did the invitation reach her so fast? Even if Amy changed her mind, how could it have been at Caroline's house fifteen minutes later?

"The envelope was sitting on my bed when I got home," Caroline was saying. "It must have come this afternoon, but I never even noticed! Isn't it cool?" She squealed with excitement. "They *do* want me after all."

Something just wasn't right about this.

"Caroline," I said carefully. "Don't you think it's a little strange that they asked you to join? You saw how weird Amy acted tonight."

Caroline sighed into the phone. "What's the big deal, Lizzy? I'm in. Why aren't you glad?"

Uh-oh. "I *am* glad," I said quickly. "But I'm worried about the Camp Fear Girls. They seem a little weird."

There was a long pause.

"I was right," Caroline said finally. "You *do* want to keep this troop all to yourself."

"What?" I cried. "No!"

"Then give me one good reason why I shouldn't go on that camp-out," Caroline demanded.

"Caroline, trust me. This is a very bad idea," I began.

"Lizzy," Caroline interrupted. "I already called Arden and told her I quit the Waynesbridge Scouts."

"You *quit* the scouts?" I repeated. Wow! Caroline was really serious about the Camp Fear Girls!

"That's right," Caroline told me. "If we don't join the Camp Fear Girls, I won't belong to any club at all. And it will be all your fault. Besides, I really want to go on this camp-out, Lizzy. And I want you to go too. It won't be any fun without you."

What could I say? *I* lied to Caroline about how cool

64

the Camp Fear Girls were. It was all my fault she quit the scouts.

"Okay, okay," I told Caroline. "We'll go together. But I'll have to ask my mom first. And besides, I never got a written invitation or a permission—"

At that second the mail slot in our front door flipped up. A yellow envelope dropped inside. I didn't have to open it. I knew what it was.

"Never mind. I think my invitation just arrived," I told Caroline.

"Then it's settled," Caroline announced. "We're both going on the camp-out."

"Yay," I said with a sinking feeling. "I can't wait."

Friday night Caroline and I stood side by side in my driveway. We had our sleeping bags, our backpacks, and our signed permission slips.

"Are you sure they're coming to pick us up?" Caroline asked, shivering a little in the night air.

"You read the invitation. It said they'd be here at eight o'clock," I replied.

Caroline slipped on her jacket. I had to help her with one of her sleeves. When I glanced up, the black van sat in the driveway.

"Whoa," Caroline murmured. "When did that pull up?"

I shrugged.

The driver was the same weird lady. She stared straight ahead while we loaded our gear into the back of the van.

"Hi, I'm Caroline." Caroline stuck her head between the front seats.

The woman stared straight ahead.

"Don't even bother," I whispered as I tugged the sliding door closed. "She won't answer you."

The old lady hit the gas, and the van peeled out of the driveway.

"Yikes!" Caroline cried, struggling to put on her seat belt.

The van whipped down River Road, then whizzed across Mill Bridge.

We zoomed down Fear Street. I flew forward and crashed into the seat in front of me as the van screeched to a halt.

I peered out the window. The van sat in front of a dark cluster of trees. The Camp Fear Girls were nowhere in sight.

"Get out," the driver growled.

"Where are we?" Caroline asked.

The woman pointed toward the thick grove of trees. "The Fear Street Woods."

Caroline clutched my arm. "Nobody told me anything about camping in *these* woods," she complained. "You know the awful stories about them, Lizzy. No birds ever sing here. People who go in don't come out."

"Do you want to go home?" I asked, hoping Caroline would say yes.

"No way!" she declared. "Let's find out where the troop is."

She leaned forward and tapped the driver on the shoulder. "Excuse me, but do you know where the troop is? We'd like to talk to them."

The driver tossed a piece of yellowed paper into the backseat. "Check the map."

"Map?" I repeated, picking it up.

"The girls are at the campsite," she said as we climbed out and unloaded our gear. "You have to find it."

Caroline glanced over my shoulder at the map. The ink had faded and the paper was torn in several places. "We can barely read this—"

Caroline didn't finish her sentence. The driver gunned the van's engine. In a flash she was gone.

"Well!" Caroline huffed. *"That* was totally rude."

I couldn't take my eyes off the Fear Street Woods. The trees stood so close together, they seemed like a solid wall.

Somehow, I couldn't shake the feeling that something was lurking inside those trees, watching us. Waiting for us to enter.

"Let's not go in." I pulled Caroline backward. "I don't want to go in."

"Oh, come on, Lizzy," she replied. "Don't be such a chicken!"

"Okay." I sighed. "Let's go."

I flicked on my flashlight's tiny beam.

Side by side, we stepped into the woods.

15

Crack!

"What was that?" Caroline aimed her flashlight at a tree.

"A twig," I whispered. "You stepped on a twig."

"I didn't," Caroline protested, blinding me with her light. "It must have been you. Lizzy, this is creepy!"

I shoved her flashlight away from my face. "Caroline, you were the one who wanted to come on this camp-out. Are you saying you want to go home now?"

"No, I am not," Caroline snapped.

We pointed our lights in front of us. Gnarled trees blocked our way. Thorny vines hung down from twisted branches and caught at our hair.

"Yeow!" Caroline cried as a branch whipped her in the face.

We walked so close together, we stepped on each other's feet. My eyes were open wide as I stared into the darkness.

Just ahead, something moved through the trees.

I locked my knees. "Did you see that?"

"Yes. What do you think it was?" Caroline whispered, barely moving her lips.

"I don't know," I groaned. "Let's just find the campsite."

Caroline held out the map and we focused our lights on the yellowed paper. "I think we're supposed to look for a stream," she murmured.

I flashed my beam in a circle around us. "I don't see a stream, do you?" I asked.

"No," Caroline replied.

Something crashed through the trees to our right.

"M-maybe we *should* forget about this camp-out," Caroline said in a shaky voice. "Maybe we *should* just go home."

"Well—okay," I agreed. I didn't want to sound too eager. But boy, was I glad Caroline changed her mind!

We turned and started back the way we came.

A few more feet, and we'll be back on Fear Street, I thought. But when I flashed my light around, I couldn't see anything but trees! And nothing looked familiar!

"Caroline," I whispered. "We must have gone the wrong way. I don't know where we are."

Caroline squeezed my hand and whimpered.

Then I heard a bubbling sound. Water! Running water!

"The stream! I think I hear it, Caroline," I told her.

We hurried forward. Branches tore at our clothes. I could hear Caroline grumbling about it. But I didn't care. I just wanted to find the campsite. Even the Camp Fear Girls weren't as creepy as this forest!

When we reached the stream, I checked the map again.

"What does it say? Where do we go now?" Caroline asked.

I squinted at the map. "I can't tell. It's all smudged."

"A light!" Caroline cried suddenly. "I see a light!"

I glanced up. She was right! Off in the distance I could just make out a faint yellow glow.

Crack! Again the sound of something moving behind us.

This time it wasn't a twig. It sounded more like a big branch. And something huge must have made it break.

No way was I turning around to find out.

"Run for it!" I screamed to Caroline. "Now!"

We took off toward the yellow light.

My pulse thundered in my ears. Brambles jabbed at me. But I didn't stop.

The light grew brighter as we ran closer.

I could see it now. A campfire!

A warm yellow campfire. In a little clearing. And girls sitting around it!

I tripped over a tree root and fell to my knees just in front of the fire.

Caroline fell next to me, gasping for breath.

Our faces were flushed. Sweat poured from my forehead as I raised my head.

The Camp Fear Girls loomed over us. They stared at Caroline and me as if we were totally nuts.

Priscilla, who was holding a guitar, spoke first. "Hey, you guys made it. Why are you so out of breath?"

I pressed my hand against my chest. It burned from running so hard. "I think someone was following us through the woods."

"Yeah. Me." Amy stepped out of the woods and into the clearing. "I saw you two back by the creek. But when I tried to catch up with you, you bolted. Are you guys on the track team, or what? You're fast!"

I glanced at Caroline. She stared back at me. Then she let out a giggle. Boy, did we feel silly!

"We got lost and I guess—well, we both freaked out," I explained. "We're not used to the woods."

"Hey, don't worry about it," Trudy told us as she pounded a tent stake into the ground. "The Fear Street Woods do that to a lot of people. But you'll get used to it."

"We did." Violet added, stirring up the campfire.

I stood up and took a closer look around the clearing. Several of the girls were making S'mores—roasted marshmallows, graham crackers, and chocolate. Priscilla was strumming her guitar. Amy had gathered wildflowers from the woods.

It all looked totally normal. Nothing creepy going on.

Maybe the Camp Fear Girls *were* just an ordinary

scout troop. The missing house on Fear Street, the way the Camp Fear Girls ignored me when I asked about Pearl—maybe I had imagined all that.

Violet handed me a S'more. "Caroline's will be ready in a minute. Make yourselves comfortable," she told us. "In a few minutes Amy is going to lead story time."

"Okay." I nodded and bit into the S'more. Mmmm! It was perfect—warm and gooshy and chocolaty. I started to relax. Maybe the camp-out was going to be fun after all!

I sat down by Caroline. She was checking out a nasty scrape she got on her knee.

Amy was stacking kindling nearby. "Where's Pearl?" I asked her. "I'd like Caroline to meet her."

Amy cocked her head and frowned. "Pearl? I don't know anyone named Pearl."

Was she kidding? I tried a laugh. "Oh, come on," I joked. "You know Pearl. Long brown braids. Purple sash."

Amy stared me straight in the eye. "There's no one in this troop named Pearl," she stated. She walked off to collect more kindling.

Uh-oh. A knot formed in my chest.

"Priscilla, where is Pearl?" I asked, trying to keep my voice steady.

Priscilla glanced at the other girls, and then shrugged. "Who's Pearl?"

I stood up and pulled Caroline away from the fire.

"Listen," I whispered. "This is very weird. I *know* there was a Pearl in this group. I met her!"

"Maybe you got her name wrong," Caroline said. "I mean, it happens sometimes."

"No!" I insisted. "I *didn't*. Something *really* strange is going on here. I—"

"Oh, stop it," Caroline interrupted. "Look around. Everyone's having a great time. Why can't you just have fun? What is wrong with you?"

Is something wrong with me? I wondered again. Am I going crazy?

"Caroline—" I tried one more time.

"Story time," Priscilla called.

"Come on, let's go." Caroline led me back to the fire. Amy perched on a rock behind her. Trudy sat beside me.

Then Amy stood up. "One hundred years ago today, a troop of scouts went into the Fear Street Woods on a camping trip."

I knew this story. I heard it at my first meeting. I guessed they were repeating it now because Caroline was new to the group.

"The girls were going to be gone for only one night," Amy went on. "But they disappeared into the woods . . . and never returned."

Hey. Wait a minute. *Pearl* was the one who told me the story at the first meeting. She *had* to exist. I couldn't have imagined her!

"Rumor has it that the girls were turned into

hideous monsters," Amy continued in an eerie voice. "And they still roam Shadyside to this day. They have rotting skin and eyeballs that fall out of their sockets." Amy seemed to really enjoy her gruesome description.

As she spoke, I made out a shadowy figure with a hideous face tiptoeing up behind Caroline.

Here comes the part where they scare Caroline with the rubber monster mask, I realized.

Amy's voice sank almost to a whisper. "If one of them ever approaches you," she warned, *"beware!* Because they are now the Camp Fear *Ghouls!"*

The shadowy figure placed her hand on Caroline's shoulder.

Caroline turned and screamed.

I burst out laughing.

Then Trudy put her hand on my right shoulder.

I turned to laugh with her.

And gasped.

Trudy's face! It was horrible!

Her flesh was rotting. A jagged bone poked through a hole in her cheek. Green pus oozed from the hole and dripped down her face.

It's just a mask, I reminded myself.

I reached out to pull the mask off Trudy's face. But my fingers sank deep into soft, putrid flesh.

It *wasn't* a mask.

Trudy was really a monster!

16

"**H**elp!" I screamed frantically.

I searched the faces around the campfire.

And then I screamed again.

They were *all* monsters!

All the Camp Fear Girls had changed into hideous, rotting creatures!

Their eyeballs bulged out of their sockets. Pus dripped from their pores. I began to choke on the smell of their decaying flesh.

Caroline dug her nails into my arm, shrieking.

Amy stood in front of us. She continued with the story.

What was the matter with her? Couldn't she see what was happening?

I jumped up and pulled Caroline to her feet. "Amy!" I cried. "Come on! We have to get away!"

Amy turned and gazed at me. Her dark eyes gleamed.

"Amy," I yelled again. "Let's get out of here! Now!"

But Amy didn't answer.

And then, as I stared at her, *she* began to change.

Her skin turned the color of pea soup. Her cheeks swelled. Larger and larger. They started to pulse.

Then the left one burst open. And something crawled out!

A worm! A fat, purple worm! It slithered across her face.

Her eyes bulged.

Her nose caved in, leaving a black hole in her face.

Caroline and I jumped to our feet.

The Camp Fear Ghouls slowly formed a circle around us. They moved closer. Tightening the circle. Closing in on us.

"Wh-what are they going to do to us?" Caroline choked out.

"I don't know!" I cried. "Let's not stick around to find out!"

I lunged at the Trudy-monster and knocked her over. Breaking the circle.

"Run, Caroline!" I cried. "Run!"

Caroline grabbed my hand. We took off for the trees.

I glanced over my shoulder. The Camp Fear Ghouls groaned. Then they began to shuffle after us.

They moved so *slowly*. We can outrun them! I thought.

It was almost as if I had spoken out loud. "You will never get away!" Amy growled.

"Don't listen to her!" I panted to Caroline.

We reached the edge of the light cast by the campfire. The woods were only a foot away. One more step and we'd be in the trees—hidden. Then we could escape.

I was in the lead. We leaped for the woods—and slammed into something solid. It felt as though I had run into a wall, headfirst.

But there was nothing there.

I rubbed my head, dazed. "What was *that?*"

"Lizzy, they're coming!" Caroline cried.

I threw myself toward the trees again.

Again I rammed into something hard. Everything swam before my eyes. Dizzy, I stumbled backward.

"What is it?" Caroline whimpered. "Why can't we get out?"

"I don't know," I croaked. "It's like there's something there—blocking our way. Only it's invisible!"

The monsters lumbered closer. They gathered around us.

"What do you want?" Caroline cried.

"Let us go!" I yelled. "Please, let us go!"

My heart thudded hard against my rib cage.

Amy raised one green, oozing finger and pointed at us. "You will never get away. You will remain with us . . . *forever!*"

17

Amy shoved her hideous face close to mine. I cringed and drew away from her.

"The campfire story is true," she rasped. "*We* are the Camp Fear Ghouls. One hundred years ago today, our troop went into these woods on a camping trip. We never went home again.

"We set up camp in this very clearing. Then we collected wood for a fire. But in the dark, no one noticed that the sticks we picked up weren't wood. They were bones. The bones of an evil man who died here!"

I sucked in my breath, horrified.

"The fire from those bones sent us all into a deep sleep," Amy continued. "When we woke up, we were . . . as you see us now. Ghouls. Camp Fear

Ghouls! Since that day we have roamed these woods. Thirteen girls—bound together forever by evil."

"But—but there were only twelve of you when I met you," I stammered. "You said I was the thirteenth. And now Pearl's gone. There are only eleven of you!"

"You're smart, Lizzy." Amy let out a horrifying laugh. "You'll be a good replacement for Rose."

"R-Rose?" I choked out.

"Yes. Rose tried to escape the Camp Fear Ghouls. We had to destroy her. We chose you to take her place."

Priscilla moved close to Caroline. She grinned. Her single tooth was covered with fuzzy green moss.

Caroline put a hand over her mouth and gagged. "Lizzy . . ." she whimpered.

It was my fault that Caroline was here. I was doomed—but maybe I could get her out of this. I took a deep breath.

"You chose me," I told the Camp Fear Ghouls. "But you didn't choose Caroline. Please let her go."

"I'm afraid we can't," Priscilla whispered.

"You see, we had to have you in our troop, Lizzy," Amy explained. "But you tried to quit when we told you your friend couldn't join. So—" She paused. "We made room for her."

Made room?

"Pearl," I whispered. "You destroyed her too."

"Right. Pearl." Amy grinned. "She was getting too bossy anyway."

"Enough talking. It is time for the initiation," Trudy announced.

My knees began to tremble.

"You must each earn three badges. One badge will test your courage," Amy said, counting on her rotting fingers. "Another will test your strength. And another, your wits."

Amy turned to the troop. "If either Lizzy or Caroline fails to survive the badge tests, they will *both* become Camp Fear Ghouls . . . forever!"

A chill raced up my spine. *If we failed to survive?*

"What if we *do* earn all our badges?" I asked.

Priscilla stepped up. A strip of torn, oozing flesh dangled from her cheek. "You won't," she told us. "But if you do—you can go."

Caroline and I squeezed each other's arms. There was hope! All we had to do was earn those badges.

Amy held up her sash. "Choose the badge you want to earn first."

Caroline and I examined the sash.

My voice shook as I explained the badges to Caroline. "The swimming badge. The rock-collecting badge. The arts and crafts badge."

"Lizzy, I'm scared. I don't want to take any of these tests. We have to go home," Caroline moaned. "Time to go home now."

"Stop it, Caroline!" I shook her by the shoulders. "We have to try to earn the badges. If we don't, we'll end up like the Camp Fear Ghouls."

Caroline's face twisted. I could see she was trying not to cry. But she nodded at me.

I studied the badges on Amy's sash.

What should we pick? Swimming, arts and crafts, or rock collecting?

Swimming could be really scary. What if they tried to drown us or something? I decided to avoid that badge for now.

That left arts and crafts and rock collecting. "I'm not the best at arts and crafts," I whispered to Caroline. "How about rock collecting? You pick up some rocks. You put them in a bag. How hard could that be?"

Caroline nodded in agreement. It seemed like the safest bet.

I took a shaky breath and said, "We're going for the rock-collecting badge."

"Rock collecting!" the ghouls whispered all together. An evil smile twisted Amy's hideous features. "Good choice," she told us. "Excellent choice!"

18

"**K**eep moving!" Trudy barked. The troop marched me and Caroline to another clearing in the Fear Street Woods.

This one had no campfire. Just dozens of large stones scattered on the ground.

Amy handed me a big cloth bag. "Fill this up with rocks."

I glanced from the bag to the rocks. That was it?

"No problem," I mouthed to Caroline.

"Pick up only these rocks," Priscilla told us, holding up a long, skinny piece of blue, glowing stone. "No others."

"You've got five minutes," Violet snapped. "Starting—now!"

The ghouls left the clearing.

The second they were out of sight, I whispered, "Quick, Caroline! They're gone! Let's make a break for it."

Caroline didn't hesitate. She turned and charged toward the trees. I followed right behind her.

But just as we hit the edge of the woods, we smacked against another invisible barrier.

Caroline cried out in pain.

"We're trapped," I groaned, rubbing my forehead.

Caroline's chin quivered. "I'm so scared, Lizzy. What do we do now?"

"The only thing we can do," I answered. "Collect rocks. But we don't have much time."

I glanced at my watch. About a minute had already passed.

Caroline crawled around the clearing on her hands and knees, pawing at the stones. "Which rocks are we supposed to collect?"

I spied some medium-size stones that seemed to glow in the dark. "Pick up those, Caroline. The bluish ones."

Caroline wrapped her hand around the one nearest her. "Yeow!" she shrieked. She dropped the rock. "It's hot!"

"Let me try." I picked up the rock.

Pain shot through my fingers. I dropped the rock. It just missed my foot. "It burned me!"

"We can't collect these rocks," Caroline cried in horror. "They burn! We're going to fail!"

"Don't say that!" I ordered.

"We're going to fail!" she repeated. "We can't do it, Lizzy—we can't!"

"We *have* to do it!" I shouted.

"They're going to turn us into ghouls!" Caroline wailed. "And there's nothing we can do to stop them!"

19

"They're not going to beat us," I cried. "I won't let them!"

I gritted my teeth and dove for another blue rock. I would hang on to it this time. Even if it fried my hand!

White heat seared my palm. I couldn't hold on!

"Ow!" I flung the rock into the air. It flew straight for Caroline.

"Look out!" I warned.

Without thinking, Caroline caught the rock with both hands.

I gasped. "Drop it, Caroline!" I yelled. "It'll burn you!"

But Caroline held on to it. She stared at it in amazement. "Lizzy, it's cold now! Ice cold!"

"No way." I strode across the clearing and grabbed the rock from Caroline.

She was right! I could hold it too—with no problem.

"That's it!" I cried. "If we toss the rocks, they cool off!" I ran to the bag and tossed the cold blue rock in. "Stay right here, Caroline. If we work together, we can do this!"

I dashed across the clearing. Hooking my toe under another burning hot rock, I kicked it into the air. Caroline caught it. She tossed it into the bag.

"Kick me another!" she yelled.

We raced against the clock, hurling one rock after another into the bag. Sweat poured down our faces. A little voice inside my head kept repeating, "You're not going to make it. You're not going to make it."

The bag filled slowly. I kicked as fast as I could. Some of the rocks flew into the air. Some didn't—and I had to try again and again.

My foot ached. My sneaker smelled charred. But I kept on. Any second the Camp Fear Ghouls would be back!

"Just a few more," Caroline huffed.

We heard a rustling sound from the woods.

"Oh, no!" Caroline gasped. "They're coming. The bag isn't full yet!"

I lunged for some rocks at the far edge of the circle. "Here come two!" I shouted, kicking them as hard as I could.

Caroline caught them both and dropped them into the bag just as the troop returned.

"Did you fail?" Amy cackled, stepping forward.

I gasped, so out of breath I could barely talk. I bent over and wheezed, "Look . . . in . . . the bag."

Amy bent and peered into the bag. She said nothing.

Caroline and I stared at each other, waiting.

Trudy stepped out of the woods. The hole in her cheek gaped open. Larger than before, I saw with horror. "Did they fail?" she asked.

Amy slowly raised her head. Her mouth twisted in a gruesome scowl. "No!" she snarled. "They did it. They filled the bag."

A low moan of disappointment echoed from the troop.

Caroline hugged me. I nearly fainted from relief.

Amy whirled to look at us. "You haven't won yet. It's time to earn your second badge."

I groaned. I couldn't hold it back.

Amy bent her horrid face close to mine. "What's the matter, Lizzy? Can't take it?" she sneered.

I forced myself to stare right into Amy's bulging eyes. "We can pass any test you give us," I replied through clenched teeth. "Right, Caroline?"

Caroline nodded shakily.

Priscilla thrust the badges in front of my face. "Choose."

I shut my eyes and pointed.

"Ooh! She picked arts and crafts," Priscilla announced. She rubbed her decaying hands together. "That's my *favorite*."

My stomach did a giant flip-flop. Oh, no. Why did Priscilla like arts and crafts so much? What horrible thing did they have in store for this test?

Violet led me and Caroline to a picnic table at the edge of the clearing. She placed two boxes in front of us. They were full of thin strips of colored plastic.

"We want you to make yourselves lanyard necklaces," Violet explained. "You know what those are, don't you?"

I knew that to make a lanyard necklace, you wove the strips of plastic together. But I didn't know *how* to do it!

I gulped. Caroline squeezed my leg under the table.

"I've done this a million times," she whispered. "I'll show you. It's just like braiding. Don't worry."

But I *was* worried. Really worried.

I stared at the box of plastic strips. Lots of people knew how to make lanyards—even if I didn't. It was too simple a test. There had to be a catch. But what was it?

"All right, girls," Priscilla said in a syrupy voice. "Get started. You have two minutes."

Caroline reached into her box. She pulled out six strips. I did the same.

So far so good.

Caroline started braiding hers, weaving the strips over and under each other. I copied her movements.

88

Then I stared at the strips in my hand. Something wasn't right. The strips seemed to move on their own!

They began slithering all over my hands.

"Caroline!" I gasped. "They're alive!"

The strips had turned into worms.

Slimy, writhing worms.

They squirmed over my palm. Between my fingers. Then they started to crawl up my arms.

"Get them off!" I screamed, shaking my arms frantically.

"Lizzy, ignore them!" Caroline ordered. "Here. Take my necklace. I'll make another."

She shoved her hand into her box again. She pulled out several new strips of plastic. She took hold of them.

The moment she started to braid them, they began to pulse. To squirm in her hands.

"They're so slippery!" she groaned, fighting to braid the writhing creatures.

"Thirty seconds!" Priscilla sang out cheerily.

"Hurry, Caroline," I whispered.

The worms crawled up Caroline's arms. Frantically she peeled them off. Added them back into the necklace. "Over. Under. Over," she muttered tensely.

I watched helplessly as she struggled.

"Ten seconds!" Priscilla laughed. "Nine . . . eight . . . seven . . . six . . ."

"There!" Caroline gasped, knotting the ends of the worms together. She slipped the slimy, wriggling necklace over her head.

89

I put mine on too. I shuddered as the worms touched my skin.

"We did it!" Caroline squealed, holding her hands in a victory sign above her head. "Yes!"

"Yes!" I tried to cheer—but my voice was suddenly cut off.

The necklace was tightening around my throat!

I reached up. I couldn't get my fingers under my writhing necklace of worms! It was choking off my air. Suffocating me.

I turned and stared, bug-eyed, at Caroline.

"Help!" I tried to scream. "Help me!"

But all that came out was a hoarse wheeze!

Caroline began to fade from my view. White lights burst before me. I was going to pass out!

"Can't breathe!" I gasped, clutching my throat. "Can't . . ."

20

I clawed desperately at my throat.

"Air," I wheezed. "Need air!"

"Ha-ha-ha-ha-ha!"

The ghouls' laughter rang in my ears.

"You'll never get that necklace off," Amy taunted. "You're ours now!"

The bursts of light swirled in front of my eyes. I slumped over the picnic table. This is it! I thought. I'm going to die.

Then I felt someone grab hold of my necklace and pull. Hard.

Caroline!

She yanked at it again. Harder this time.

Snap!

The necklace broke in half.

Cool air rushed into my burning lungs!

I fell to the ground, sucking in huge mouthfuls of air.

I raised my head to thank Caroline. But she had fallen against the picnic table.

Both hands were at her throat.

Her face was turning an awful shade of blue.

Caroline's necklace! *She* was choking too! Her mouth opened and closed as she struggled for air.

I leaped to my feet and stumbled toward her. My fingers grabbed for the deadly necklace. I pulled with all my strength.

Snap!

Caroline's necklace broke.

She leaned forward, gasping.

"Caroline," I whispered. "You saved me. You saved my life!"

Amy lunged between us. She looked furious. There was an evil red glare in her hideous eyes.

"Enough of this!" Her voice boomed through the woods. "Time for your final test."

"Oh, no!" Caroline groaned.

Amy pointed through the trees. A huge pool of shiny black water shimmered there.

"To earn your swimming badge," she growled, "you have to swim across Fear Lake!"

21

Fear Lake was blacker than any lake I had ever seen. Even the people in Waynesbridge knew that no one ever swims in Fear Lake. The lake is icy. It never gets warm. Even in the middle of summer.

And that wasn't all. People said the cold wasn't the worst thing about Fear Lake. But no one ever told me what the worst thing *was*.

I shivered. What horrible things might be lurking in the freezing water?

The Camp Fear Ghouls led us to the shore. Caroline and I took off our shoes and stuck our toes into the lake.

I jumped back. Waves of cold shot through my body. "Ice!" I gasped. "It's ice!"

"Lizzy," Caroline rasped, rubbing her foot to get it

warm. "That lake is too cold. We won't last five minutes in there!"

I glanced over my shoulder at the Camp Fear Ghouls. They stood in a line, watching us.

"We have to swim it," I whispered back. "If we don't, we join them."

"Let's get this over with," Amy growled.

The ghouls moved toward us. With their rotting hands, they shoved us forward.

Caroline and I stumbled waist deep into the pitch-black water.

I gasped. "It's so c-c-cold!"

"Oh!" Caroline moaned. "This is terrible!"

"We have to g-g-go," I cried through chattering teeth. "Have to s-swim t-to the other s-side."

Don't think about the cold, I ordered myself. Just swim!

I raised my hand over my head to take my first stroke.

What was that?

Something brushed my leg.

I spun in a circle, frantically treading water.

"Lizzy? What's the matter?" Caroline cried.

"Something touched me," I gasped, trying to see into the lake's murky depths.

There! I felt it again. Something brushing up against me.

"Caroline!" I yelled, thrashing my legs as hard as I could. "Something's in the lake!"

I jerked right. Then left. Trying to peer into the water.

I felt something wind around my ankle. Pulling me down into the water. "Help!" I screamed.

"What is it?" Caroline wailed.

"I don't know! I can't see anything!"

Desperately, I kicked—and freed my leg from whatever held it.

Then I took off for the other side.

Caroline swam right behind me.

My pulse thudded in my ears. The only other sound I heard was the splash our arms made as we cut through the water.

We swam as fast as we could—and all of a sudden the opposite shore was in sight. Yes!

Just a little ways more, I thought. I swam even faster.

Then I heard the scream.

"Help, Lizzy!" Caroline cried out. "It's got me!"

I whipped my head around.

Just in time to see Caroline sink under the surface of Fear Lake.

22

"*Caroline!*" I screamed.

The surface of the water was glassy. There was no sign of Caroline anywhere.

I sucked as much air into my lungs as I could—and dove under the black water!

I couldn't see a thing. I swam forward blindly, feeling for Caroline.

She wasn't there.

I turned and swam the other way, swiping at the water in front of me. The cold shot through me.

Where is she? I wondered frantically. I can't stay in here much longer. I'll freeze!

I reversed direction again, blindly searching. But I couldn't stay under for another second. My lungs burned. I had to go up for air!

With a kick, I shot to the surface.

I sucked in another huge breath, ready to go down again. But then something burst through the surface. Just a few feet away.

Caroline!

"Lizzy!" she sputtered. "It's . . . got . . . me!"

"*What's* got you?" I yelled.

"Get help!" Caroline screamed.

Then she disappeared under the water again.

I took off for the shore.

Get help, I thought. Have to get help.

My whole body was numb with cold. That's why I didn't feel the creature wrapped around my ankle.

I began to wade ashore—and felt a tug on my leg.

I glanced down—and saw it.

A giant, scaly black tentacle, winding its way up my thigh.

Dragging me back into the water!

23

"**N**o!" I cried.

I shook my leg. The slimy tentacle held on tight, dragging me down. I clawed at the shore. Grasping at sticks. Roots. Anything!

But it was useless. The more I struggled, the harder the lake monster pulled.

The tentacle rose higher. Wrapped itself around my waist.

I could see the creature now. Some sort of hideous octopus. With throbbing veins pulsing against its slimy skin.

I beat at the tentacle with my fists. Trying to struggle free.

The creature tightened its grip.

Three more tentacles shot up from the water. Swaying wildly. Grasping for my body.

Whack! My flailing hand slammed against something on the ground. Something sharp.

My fingers closed around a jagged rock.

I lifted it—and pounded it against the creature's tentacle. Pounded as hard as I could.

A high-pitched howl of pain echoed through the Fear Street Woods. Fear Lake bubbled and foamed.

The tentacle around my waist loosened.

Then it slid back into the lake—and Caroline surfaced!

Sputtering and coughing, she swam for the shore. I waded out to meet her. The two of us collapsed on the muddy bank.

My body throbbed where the creature grabbed me. I ached all over. But I was alive. And we had made it across the lake!

Amy and the other Camp Fear Ghouls stepped out of the woods and stood in a semicircle around us. I could barely raise my head to look at them.

"We did it," I croaked. "We earned all our badges. Now we're going."

"Oh!" Amy said with an apologetic smile. "Did we say if you passed all your tests we would *let you go?*"

I bolted up. I stared Amy straight in the eye. "Yes!" I cried. "That's what you said!"

"Oh, nooo," Amy cooed. "What we meant to say was—if you passed all your tests, we *wouldn't* let you go!"

24

"**N**o!" Caroline shrieked. "You have to let us go. That was the deal!"

"Deal?" Amy repeated. "The Camp Fear Ghouls don't make deals!"

Priscilla placed one hand over her heart. "It's time for the crossing-over ceremony."

Trudy leaned her rotting face close to mine and whispered, "You will now become Camp Fear Ghouls—for all eternity!"

The hideous ghouls herded us back to the campfire. They shoved us to the ground. Then they moved in a slow circle around us—and began to sing.

> "Thirteen girls went off to camp;
> The woods were dark, the ground was damp."

My heart hammered in my chest. I had to do something. Before it was too late.

But the song. It was so soothing. . . .

I felt myself beginning to sway back and forth.

No! I thought. I have to get us out of here!

I tried to stand. But I couldn't! I couldn't do anything—except listen.

The troop continued singing.

"Thirteen families dressed in black.
Thirteen girls who never came back."

They're putting us in some kind of trance, I realized. I can't let them!

I pressed my hands to my ears. "Don't listen, Caroline!" I shouted.

I squeezed my eyes closed as the ghouls sang about rotting eyes and hungry worms.

I tried to think of school. My family. My room at home. But no matter what I did, my mind kept coming back to the words of the ghouls' song.

"Thirteen bodies in the ground.
Thirteen heads that never were found."

A dark, evil feeling filled my body. The same feeling I had during Prank Night. It filled my head. It clouded my brain.

Bad thoughts. Evil thoughts formed in my mind.

Beside me, Caroline moaned.

I turned to her—and in the flickering firelight, I saw her face . . . changing!

Her eyes bulged. They began to turn yellow. Then they rolled up into her head.

Her lips curled into an ugly sneer.

A gaping sore opened on her forehead. Her skin began to wither and peel away.

"No!" I screamed at the Camp Fear Ghouls. "I won't let you do this!"

I lunged for Caroline. I grabbed her by the shoulders and shook her—hard!

"Don't listen to it!" I ordered Caroline. "Think of something else. Sing a different song!"

The ghouls' song seemed to get louder. Faster.

"Thirteen girls who want revenge."

Desperately, I sang the first thing that popped into my head.

"We're the very best of friends!" I shouted over the ghouls' song. "We'll be best friends till the end!"

Caroline blinked at me.

"Sing, Caroline! Sing! B-E-S-T, best friends!" I screamed. Then I started the whole thing again. "We're the very best of friends! We'll be best friends till the end."

"B-E-S-T," Caroline murmured through swollen lips. "Best friends."

"That's it!" I yelled. "Come on, Caroline, one more time!"

Caroline joined in. We sang our song again.

Was it working?

I peered at Caroline's hideous face.

As I stared, the sore on her forehead began to fade. Then it vanished!

It was working. The cheer really was working!

The ghouls stopped singing.

"No!" Amy screeched. "Noooo!"

Caroline and I sang the cheer again—this time bellowing it at the top of our lungs. "We're the very best of friends—"

"Stop!" the ghouls wailed.

"We'll be best friends till the end."

Caroline's face returned to normal.

She grinned at me and shouted, "B-E-S-T, best—"

She didn't finish. Her smile faded. She stared over my shoulder in horror.

I whipped around to the campfire behind me.

My mouth suddenly went dry. "Whoa," I whispered.

There, floating above the flames, was Pearl!

25

Pearl hovered over us. She wore her troop uniform—purple sash and all.

But I could see right through her to the trees surrounding the clearing.

Pearl wasn't a ghoul anymore. She was a ghost!

"You have failed!" she bellowed.

"No!" I shrieked. "We passed!"

"Not you." Pearl slowly turned her head to stare at the troop. *"You!"* She pointed a ghostly finger at Amy and the Camp Fear Ghouls. "You have all failed!"

Amy shrank back in fear. "Wh-what are you doing here?" she stammered. "We destroyed you. Just like we destroyed Rose!"

Pearl's voice boomed over the trees. "Fool! You destroyed my body. But you cannot destroy *me!*

I am the leader. I must *always* be part of the thirteen!"

"I told you we couldn't get rid of her," Trudy whispered to Amy. "But you wouldn't listen."

"Shut up!" Amy growled.

Pearl floated closer to Amy. "Amy is the most to blame. Because of her, we do not have the correct number of members. But you all did as Amy told you. You all broke the rules." Pearl suddenly bellowed, *"Now you all must pay!"*

Amy dropped to her knees. "No!"

"Yes!" Pearl pointed her skeletal hand at Amy and ordered, "Camp Fear Ghouls, COUNT OFF!"

Amy clasped her hands together. "Please, don't make me!"

Pearl sucked in a huge breath of air, then roared, "ONE!"

The Camp Fear Ghouls stared up at Pearl. Total fear showed on their disgusting faces.

What were they afraid of? What would happen if they counted off?

Pearl floated closer to Amy. "I said, ONE!"

Amy covered her head and moaned, "TWO!"

"THREE!" Priscilla whimpered.

"FOUR!" Trudy cried.

Thunder rumbled in the distance. The ghouls kept counting.

"FIVE!"

"SIX!"

I watched their faces, trying to put it together.

There were supposed to be thirteen girls in the troop. That was the key, I knew. But the key to what?

The thunder crashed again. Closer to camp this time.

Violet was the last of the ghouls to count off. "TWELVE!"

The troop turned to face Caroline and me.

Pearl hovered over me. "Say it!" she ordered.

"THIRTEEN!" I shouted.

Lightning struck a tree a few feet away. The night sky exploded with light.

"Now you!" Pearl pointed at Caroline.

I turned to Caroline. She stood frozen, her eyes wide with fear.

"Caroline," I whispered. "Say it."

Caroline stared blankly ahead, shivering.

I grabbed her by the shoulders and shook her. "Say it, Caroline!" I ordered. "Say 'fourteen!'"

But Caroline didn't say a thing.

26

"**S**ay it!" I screamed. "Say it!"

Caroline's whole body trembled. Her eyes remained fixed on Pearl.

I shook her again. "Caroline! You have to do it! Please! You have to yell—"

Caroline blinked her eyes. "FOURTEEN!" she shouted.

Crraaaack! A lightning bolt sizzled down into the camp.

Dazzling white light flashed all around. The ground heaved under me. Caroline and I flew through the air. *Whump!* We hit the ground with a bone-jarring thud.

Amy and the other Camp Fear Ghouls screeched in agony. I rolled over and peered toward them.

But there was no one there.

The Camp Fear Ghouls had disappeared.

"They're gone," I gasped. "The ghouls are gone!"

"Not all of them," Caroline corrected me. She clutched my arm and pointed.

Pearl remained, floating above the flames of the campfire.

She smiled a ghoulish grin at us. "Fourteen!" she howled. "We can't have fourteen girls. That's breaking the rules!"

Then she shot skyward—and vanished into the night.

The campfire went out.

We were in total darkness.

Then a yellow cone of light shone in my eyes. "Oh, no!" I moaned. Caroline and I clutched at each other. What now?

"Lizzy?" a familiar voice called.

"Lizzy, where are you?" another voice called.

I let go of Caroline. "Mom? Dad?"

I leaped to my feet and ran to my parents.

"Mom! Dad!" I squealed. "What are you doing here?"

"The Weather Service reported severe thunderstorms in the area," Mom explained. "We just didn't think it was a good idea for you to camp in these woods tonight. We came to take you home."

"I'm never camping in these woods again!" I said. I flung my arms around her neck.

"Lizzy, where is the rest of your troop?" Dad asked me, frowning.

"They—uh—just left," I replied.

Well, it was true. Sort of.

"That's why we were so happy to see you," Caroline added.

We followed my parents out of the woods to our car.

As we drove toward Mill Bridge, Mom turned in her seat. "Oh, Lizzy, I almost forgot. This came in the mail for you."

She passed an envelope over the back of the seat. I opened it and read the letter out loud. "Join the Shadyside Drama Club."

Hmm, I thought. A drama club sounds fun. Maybe . . .

"Don't even think about it." Caroline yanked the letter out of my hands. She tore it into little pieces and tossed them out the window. "We've had enough of clubs—"

"And Fear Street," I added, watching the bits of paper float away.

"Right!" Caroline slung her arm around my shoulder. "No more Fear Street. No more clubs. From now on, it's just you and me."

"Oh! Look, girls," Mom called. She pointed out the window.

I peered out. And gasped.

"Hi, girls!" The Camp Fear Ghouls' driver stood on Mill Bridge. Waving. "See you tomorrow night!"

Are you ready for another walk
down Fear Street?
Turn the page for a terrifying
sneak preview.

R.L.STINE'S
GHOSTS of FEAR STREET ® #19

THREE EVIL WISHES

Coming mid-March 1997

Jesse stared at me. "You really want to go in *there? In Fear Lake?*"

The lake, just like the Fear Street Woods, had a pretty creepy reputation.

"No. I don't *want* to go in," I replied. "But what choice do we have? We have to get our backpacks."

Jesse knew we *had* no choice. We had to go in.

We pulled off our shoes and socks and rolled up our jeans as high as they would go.

"That water is going to be freezing," Jesse warned.

I hoped he was wrong. I walked up to the edge of the lake and peered in. Above, the sun slid behind clouds again. The water was so dark and cloudy, I could barely see the bottom. I dipped my big toe in for a half a second—and drew it back.

Cold. Very cold.

"I can't believe the Burger brothers did this to us! I hate them for throwing our packs in Fear Lake!" I cried. "I *wish* we could pay them back!"

I took a deep breath and waded into the cold water, moving as fast as I could. The cold took my breath away. I gasped. And shivered. And gasped again. I wrapped my arms around my body to keep warm.

"Whooooa!" I shouted. Did something slimy brush up against my leg? It sure felt like it. And in Fear Lake, I wasn't taking any chances. I started to wade back to the shore—fast.

"Jesse! Something's here—in the water!" I shouted. "Something *alive!*"

Jesse grabbed my wrist. "Yeah. They're called *fish.*"

Together we walked a few more steps into the dark, cold water. Then, in front of me, something splashed to the surface.

A fish?

No. It bobbed in slow circles just under the surface. What could it be?

"Got it!" Jesse cried.

He yanked his backpack up from the water. "Yuccck!" he moaned. The backpack was covered in black mud.

I lowered my eyes to the water. The strange object began to bob toward me!

A voice in the back of mind told me to get out of the lake right away. To stay away from that thing in the water.

I should have listened.

But instead, I took a step forward. I squeezed my eyes shut—and reached my hand out to grab it.

I wrapped my fingers around the object. It felt slick and hard. I pulled it out of the water and held it up to examine it.

A bottle?

Yes. It *was* a bottle. An ordinary, brown, glass bottle with a cork in it.

I let out a sigh of relief. Nothing spooky or weird about a bottle. Someone probably threw it in the lake after a picnic.

I was about to drop the bottle back into the water, when I noticed something strange about it. It should have been cold—but it felt warm. Warmer than my hand.

I held onto the bottle as I hunted for my backpack.

"Found it," I called to Jesse, who was already on shore.

I dredged up my backpack. Gross. It was muddy and covered with clumps of soggy green weeds.

I waded back to shore with the bottle and my backpack. "Hey, Jess. Check out this bottle. It feels warm and—"

The bottle jerked in my hand!

I nearly dropped it.

Did something *move* inside it? Was something *alive* in there?

I tried to peer through the brown glass. But it was thick and dirty. I couldn't see a thing.

Get a grip, Hannah! I thought to myself. Nothing could be living in this old bottle.

I turned to Jesse. He frowned as he stared at his mud-soaked backpack. "Totally ruined," he moaned, shaking his head. "Dad is going to freak. He'll totally freak."

I began to answer Jesse, when I felt my hand grow warmer. The bottle was heating up! It jerked in my hand again. Harder this time.

Something very weird was going on here. I set the bottle down in the grass. I didn't want to hold on to it another second.

"Hey, what's that?" Jesse asked, nodding his head toward the bottle.

"What does it look like, Brain? It's a bottle I found in the lake."

"Wow. It looks *really* old," he said, bending down to examine it.

He reached his hand out and picked it up. "Yuck! It's . . . it's *hot!*"

So I wasn't going crazy! There really *was* something strange about that bottle.

Jesse held it up to the sun. He squinted his eyes, trying to peer inside.

"Is there a note inside? People always do that in the movies."

"I found this in the *lake,* Jesse. People don't throw bottles with notes in them in a lake. They throw them in the ocean to see how far they will travel."

"Hey, maybe it's got money inside!" Jesse cried. He

tried even harder to see through the dark brown glass. He shook the bottle.

"Oh, yeah, people are *always* throwing bottles filled with money into the lake." I scowled at my brother. "Look, just put it down, okay? We're soaked. We have to go home and change."

Jesse ignored me as he squinted at the bottle. "Hey, it feels as if it's getting even warmer."

"Jess, put it down!" I insisted. My voice quivered.

"What's your problem, Hannah? It's just a bottle." He turned it around in his hand, inspecting every inch. "I'm going to open it."

"No! Wait!" I cried. I grabbed the bottle from him. "There's something written on the side. Maybe it's important."

"If you say so." Jesse sighed.

A yellow label clung to the side of the bottle. The letters on it were so faded, I could barely make them out.

"'DANGER,'" I read out loud. "'DO NOT OPEN.'"

The bottle began to vibrate in my hand.

I jumped.

This was definitely *not* my imagination.

I dropped the bottle back onto the ground and kicked it away. "This bottle is bad news. I'm not opening it! I don't even want it near me!"

It sat there on its side in the grass. Then, slowly, it rolled back to me.

"Did you see that, Jesse?" I whispered. "It—it moved on its own!"

Jesse groaned and picked the bottle up again. "It just rolled. Bottles do that."

"Let's go," I urged. "I told you what it says on the label. We are *not* supposed to open this bottle."

Jesse took hold of the cork. "That's stupid."

"No, Jesse, *don't!*"

I reached out to swipe the bottle from him.

Too late.

He grasped the cork and tugged it out of the bottle.

About R. L. Stine

R. L. Stine, the creator of *Ghosts of Fear Street,* has written almost 100 scary novels for kids. The *Ghosts of Fear Street* series, like the *Fear Street* series, takes place in Shadyside and centers on the scary events that happen to people on Fear Street.

When he isn't writing, R. L. Stine likes to play pinball on his very own pinball machine and explore New York City with his wife, Jane, and fifteen-year-old son, Matt.

WIN A TRIP TO MEET

R·L·STINE

...IF YOU DARE!

You could win an exciting weekend in New York City and have lunch with R.L. Stine

1 GRAND PRIZE: A WEEKEND (3 DAY/2 NIGHT) TRIP TO NEW YORK CITY TO MEET R.L. STINE

10 First Prizes: Walkman and an autographed "Ghosts of Fear Street" Audiobook

20 Second Prizes: Autographed "Ghosts of Fear Street" T-Shirt

30 Third Prizes: Autographed "Ghosts of Fear Street" Audiobook

50 Fourth Prizes: Autographed "Ghosts of Fear Street" Book

100 Fifth Prizes: "Ghosts of Fear Street" Sticker

Complete the official entry form and send to:
Pocket Books, GOFS Sweepstakes
1230 Avenue of the Americas, New York, NY 10020

Name_____(Child)

Birthdate_____/_____/_____

Name_____(Parent)

Address _____

City_____State_____Zip_____

Phone (_____)_____

See back for official rules   1302 (1 of 2)

POCKET BOOKS/"GOFS AUDIO" SWEEPSTAKES
Sweepstakes Official Rules:

1. No Purchase Necessary. Enter by mailing the completed Official Entry Form (no copies allowed) or by mailing a 3" x 5" card with your name and address to the Pocket Books/GOFS Sweepstakes,13th Floor, 1230 Avenue of the Americas, NY, NY 10020. Entries must be received by 6/30/97. Not responsible for lost, late, stolen, illegible, mutilated, incomplete, postage due or misdirected entries or mail or for typographical errors in the entry form or rules. Enter as often as you wish, but one entry per envelope. Winners will be selected at random from all eligible entries received in a drawing to be held on or about 7/1/97.

2. Prizes: One Grand Prize: A weekend (three day/two night) trip for up to four persons (the winning minor, one parent or legal guardian and two guests) including round-trip coach airfare from the major U.S. airport nearest the winner's residence to New York City, ground transportation or car rental in New York City, meals, two nights in a hotel (one room, occupancy for four) and lunch with R.L. Stine (approx. retail value $3500.000, trip must be taken on the date specified by Simon & Schuster, Inc.), Ten First Prizes: Walkman and Autographed "Ghosts of Fear Street" Audiobook (approx. retail value $40.00) Twenty Second Prizes: Autographed "Ghosts of Fear Street" T-shirt (approx. retail value $20.00 each), Thirty Third Prizes: Autographed "Ghosts of Fear Street" Audiobook (approx. retail value $7.95 each), Fifty Fourth Prizes: Autographed "Ghosts of Fear Street" Book (approx. retail value: $3.99) One Hundred Fifth Prizes: "Ghosts of Fear Street" Sticker (approx. retail value: $1.00)

3. The sweepstakes is open to residents of the U.S. and Canada, excluding Quebec, not older than fourteen as of 6/30/97. Proof of age required to claim prize. Prizes will be awarded to the winner's parent or legal guardian. Void in Puerto Rico and wherever prohibited or restricted by law. Simon & Schuster, Inc., Parachute Press, Inc., their respecitve officers, directors, shareholders, employees, suppliers, parents, subsidiaries, affiliates, agencies, sponsors, participating retailers, and persons connected with the use, marketing or conduct of this sweepstakes and their families living in the same household, are not eligible.

4. One prize per person or household. Prizes are not transferable and may not be substituted except by sponsor, in event of unavailability, in which case a prize of equal or greater value will be awarded. All prizes will be awarded. The odds of winning a prize depend upon the number of eligible entries received.

5. If a winner is a Canadian resident, then he/she must correctly answer a skill-based question administered by mail.

6. All expenses on receipt and use of prize including Federal, state and local taxes are the sole responsibility of the winners. Winners will be notified by mail. Winners may be required to execute and return an Affidavit of Eligibility and Release and all other legal documents which the sweepstakes sponsor may require (including a W-9 tax form) within 15 days of receipt of notification or an alternate winner will be selected.

7. Winners irrevocably grant Pocket Books, Parachute Press, Inc. and Simon & Schuster Audio the worldwide right, for no additional consideration, to use their names, photographs, likenesses, and entries for any advertising, promotion, marketing and publicity purposes relating to this promotional contest or otherwise without further compensation to or permission from the entrants, except where prohibited by law.

8. Winners agree that Simon & Schuster Inc., Parachute Press, Inc., their respective officers, directors, shareholders, employees, suppliers, parents, subsidiaries, affiliates, agencies, sponsors, participating retailers, and persons connected with the use, marketing or conduct of this sweepstakes, shall have no liability in connection with the collection, acceptance or use of the prizes awarded herein.

9. By participating in this sweepstakes, entrants agree to be bound by these rules and the decisions of the judges and sweepstakes sponsors, which are final in all matters relating to the sweepstakes.

10. For a list of major prize winners, (available after 7/11/97) send a stamped, self-addressed envelope to Prize Winners, Pocket Books/GOFS Sweepstakes, 13th Floor, 1230 Avenue of the Americas, NY, NY 10020.

COMING IN MARCH 1997

THE FIRST-EVER GHOSTS OF FEAR STREET® AUDIOBOOK

THREE EVIL WISHES

A never-before-published
Ghosts of Fear Street® title

Not available as a book until April!